Children of Darkness

A Tragi-comedy in Three Acts

by Edwin Justus Mayer

A SAMUEL FRENCH ACTING EDITION

FOUNDED 1830

New York Hollywood London Toronto

SAMUELFRENCH.COM

CHILDREN OF DARKNESS

STORY OF THE PLAY

Among the paying guests of Mr. Snap, under-sheriff of London and Middlesex, and chief jailer of Newgate prison in 1725, are the Count La Ruse and Jonathan Wild, thieves; Mr. Cartwright, a young poet, and Lord Wainwright, poisoner. Laetitia, the jailer's daughter, loves La Ruse desperately, and when he seeks to break her hold upon him, takes up with Mr. Cartwright by way of bringing La Ruse back. La Ruse and Mr. Snap conspire to rob Jonathan Wild the day of his hanging, on pretense of buying him a pardon. With freedom in sight, La Ruse, convinced by Laetitia of his worthlessness and the hopelessness of any attempted reform, takes his own life, leaving the money he has stolen to free the poet. Laetitia falls then to Lord Wainwright.

Copy of program of first performance of "Children of Darkness," a tragi-comedy in three acts by Edwin Justus Mayer. Produced by Kenneth Macgowan and Joseph Verner Reed at the Biltmore Theatre, New York:

CAST OF CHARACTERS

MR. SNAP, *Under-Sheriff of London and Middlesex*
—Walter Kingsford
FIRST BAILIFF .... *Albert Bees*
MR. CARTWRIGHT .... *J. Kerby Hawkes*
MR. FIERCE .... *Richard Menefee*
JONATHAN WILD, THE GREAT .... *Charles Dalton*
COUNT LA RUSE .... *Basil Sydney*
LAETITIA .... *Mary Ellis*
LORD WAINWRIGHT .... *Eugene Powers*
BAILIFFS .... *Joseph Skinner, William Plunket*

Acts I, II and III: *Room in the house of Mr. Snap, adjoining Newgate Prison, London.*

Staged by Edwin Justus Mayer

DESCRIPTION OF CHARACTERS

MR. SNAP: *Old and myopic.*

CARTWRIGHT: *He is young, straight, clear-eyed.*

MR. FIERCE: *A muscular ruffian, bare-headed, bare-throated and coatless.*

JONATHAN WILD: *A burly, boisterous man of forty.*

LA RUSE: *A polished, cynical, middle-aged man.*

LAETITIA: *She is twenty-nine, a ravishing woman; vital to the excess of carnality.*

LORD WAINWRIGHT: *A nobleman whose face is a chronic deadly white. His teeth are his most prominent feature; they protrude over his lip. His eyes are his least prominent feature; they are of that peculiar gray which seems to diffuse itself, the better to see. In his bearing, he has the genuine distinction of his class; and his speech is tinged with a hesitancy which is contradicted by the decisiveness of his thoughts.*

Children Of Darkness

ACT ONE

*A room on the top floor of Mr. Snap's house, close
by Newgate Prison.*
*There is a barred window Right Center at
back and another in Left wall of hall off Center. The city can be seen lying vaguely away.*
*At the Left rear corner is a fireplace, but as
the season is late spring, it is not in use. A fine
old tall clock in Right rear corner that strikes
the hour and the half hour; a sofa under Right
Center window. A door Center. A door at the
Right front leads into a hall. A door Left.*
*The room has been designed for living, but
latterly someone has been using it as an office;
for a table at the Left Center, where the clear-
est light falls, is covered with a disorderly array
of ledgers, papers, an ink-pot, quill pens, etc.
Chairs Right, Left and back of table; also
Right Center and below fireplace.*

MR. SNAP, *old and myopic, walks up and down the
room. He looks at the clock, then at the* R. *door,
as if expecting someone. At length, a* BAILIFF
enters R.

MR. SNAP. Well, well.
BAILIFF. We've brought the boy from the jail, sir.

MR. SNAP. Never mind the boy, knave! Are the gallows prepared for Mr. Wild, sir?

BAILIFF. Aye, sir.

MR. SNAP. Even if Wild don't swing—there will always be a rogue to take his place.

BAILIFF. Aye, sir—so there will.

MR. SNAP. You said you'd brought the boy from the jail. Where is he?

BAILIFF. He's in the hall.

MR. SNAP. Fetch him to me! But wait. You know all the rogues in London. You must know Mr. Fierce.

BAILIFF. Aye, one of Wild's gang. He tumbled me downstairs—when we took Wild.

MR. SNAP. 'Tis your chance to tumble him, for he comes this morning to visit Wild. You will seize him at the door and bring him here—but not before you've put the irons on him, knave. Now let me see the boy. (BAILIFF *goes out* R. MR. SNAP *whistles cheerily. The* BAILIFF *returns, with a comrade.* CARTWRIGHT *walks between them; he is young, straight, clear-eyed, but obviously depressed.)* Your servant, Mr. Cartwright. *(Dismisses* BAILIFF*)* I am Mr. Snap of the jail.

CARTWRIGHT. *(Wearily)* Why am I brought here, Mr. Snap?

MR. SNAP. You'll be delighted to hear, Mr. Cartwright. *(The* BAILIFF *goes.)* Sit down, Mr. Cartwright, sit down! *(Crosses to chair* R.C.*)* That is, if you can on such a morning! I had my walk this morning— I would not have missed my walk on such a morning! *(Crosses back to* C.*)*

CARTWRIGHT. I would have missed mine gladly. *(Sits* R.C.*)*

MR. SNAP. *(Chuckling unpleasantly)* Would you? Would you? Because they walked you to Newgate? You're in the doldrums, Mr. Cartwright. Because you're jailed? At your age I had been jailed a dozen times. Why, 'tis only the effeminate and useless young who keep out of jail completely; the young who have never been in jail are a disgrace to their youth, sir.

CARTWRIGHT. Perhaps. *(Points towards prison, off* L.*)* But 'tis monstrous that men should treat men so—

MR. SNAP. I guessed at once you were held for debt! It takes a rogue to pay his bills honestly; a gentleman is much too busy accumulating more such, to pay such as he has accumulated.

CARTWRIGHT. I was gulled into signing a paper. But why have you brought me here, Mr. Snap?

MR. SNAP. Why, sir, because I guessed you would far rather be held here than down in the jail.

CARTWRIGHT. But I was consigned to the jail, by writ.

MR. SNAP. Yes, but I've power there, Mr. Cartwright. I'd not have you here were you not a gentleman. I've a daughter, a daughter I prize, a daughter who, I may say, possesses all the domestic virtues! I'd not expose her to the riff-raff—no, not for any sum. You shall be held here, sir.

CARTWRIGHT. *(Overjoyed)* This is more than kind of you, Mr. Snap.

MR. SNAP. Of course, you have some small fees to disburse through me.

CARTWRIGHT. *(Dismayed)* Fees!

MR. SNAP. What did you expect, sir? You've said yourself the King's Writ consigned you to Newgate —not to my house!

CARTWRIGHT. I thought you brought me here from kindness—not to be fee'd!

MR. SNAP. *(Mistakes* CARTWRIGHT'S *innocence for impudence)* Do not put me out of temper with such remarks, Mr. Cartwright. What! Must kindness be divorced from profit? I will have you know, Mr. Cartwright, your remark has lowered my spirits—they droop, they droop perceptibly! Perhaps after all you were best returned to the jail.

CARTWRIGHT. *(Terrified)* Anywhere but there! How much is requisite?

MR. SNAP. For ten guineas you may enjoy the entire privacy of this floor.

CARTWRIGHT. I have but five pounds to my name. *(Takes out money.)*

MR. SNAP. But you can procure five pounds additional? (CARTWRIGHT *shakes his head hopelessly.)* Have you no friend? No mistress?

CARTWRIGHT. No.

MR. SNAP. Pray, what is your means of livelihood, then?

CARTWRIGHT. *(Defiantly, for he has learned that his proud avowal often brings derision)* I am a poet.

MR. SNAP. *(Sadly disillusioned)* What, a poet! I thought you were a gentleman. On my word, sir, you have a better air than the vulgarity of your trade allows. But hold—you say you are a poet—and have no mistress?

CARTWRIGHT. *(Quietly, resentful)* Every poet has the same mistress.

MR. SNAP. *(Jeeringly)* Is she beautiful, poet?

CARTWRIGHT. So beautiful—that she destroys my own ugliness.

MR. SNAP. Is she rich, poet?

CARTWRIGHT. She owns all seed—all harvests.

MR. SNAP. And yet she cannot provide you with five pounds more! On my word, your fol-de-rol-dol has put me in a mood to do the handsome thing. I will sell you the privacy of the floor for what money you have. *(He takes the money.)*

(A loud HUBBUB of blows, cries and oaths is heard in the hall, R. MR. FIERCE, a muscular ruffian, bare-headed, bare-throated and coatless, is dragged in by two BAILIFFS; to C. Although

*he is manacled, they have a difficult time hold-
ing him.)*

MR. FIERCE. *(Bellowing at* MR. SNAP*)* Call off
your terriers—your male wenches!

MR. SNAP. Mr. Fierce, I believe. I have had the
pleasure before, have I not? *(He takes a document
from his pocket)* We have a warrant for your ar-
rest.

MR. FIERCE. Damn your eyes for a lying cuckold!

MR. SNAP. *(Merrily)* My wife is dead, sir.

MR. FIERCE. She's cuckolding you then in hell!

MR. SNAP. *(Amiably)* It is my duty to warn you,
Mr. Fierce, that anything you say may be used
against you. You are charged with the grand larceny
of a silver locket from one Lady Margaret Steb-
bins, since deceased.

MR. FIERCE. Silver locket. *(The words have
stunned him; he asks in a curious voice)* Who swore
to the complaint? (MR. SNAP *offers him the warrant. Sullenly)* I can't read.

MR. SNAP. *(Reads from the document)* Jonathan
Wild made the complaint.

MR. FIERCE. *(Quivering)* Jonathan Wild!

MR. SNAP. He is witness that you offered him the
stolen property, which he declined.

MR. FIERCE. Declined! 'Twas he who told me of
the locket—where to filch it—

MR. SNAP. Aye, Mr. Wild usually knows where
other people's valuables lie.

MR. FIERCE. And that he'd get rid of it for me!
He has it now, for disposal!

MR. SNAP. I doubt if you can prove that. *(He
hands the warrant to one of the* BAILIFFS*)* Take him
to the jail.

MR. FIERCE. *(Awakening from his stupor—fighting savagely)* He's here in this house— By God, I'll
kill him—the double-cheating bastard—of a French

dancing-master— I'll chew him to pieces— I'll bathe in his blood— *(A murderous blow subdues* FIERCE; *he is dragged away out* R.*)*

CARTWRIGHT. Horrible. Wild has used this unfortunate man and then betrayed him.

MR. SNAP. And betrayed a thousand other tools— and yet he sniffles, prates of his honour and the principle of the thing. Let me warn you against Mr. Wild, and against a precious friend of his, also held here, who calls himself Count La Ruse. Put your faith in me, sir.

CARTWRIGHT. 'Twas published Wild was sentenced to death.

MR. SNAP. He'll swing any day, now. There is no crime so low he hasn't had a hand in it, and here, where his talents are somewhat circumscribed, he robs La Ruse, La Ruse robs him—

CARTWRIGHT. And you rob both of them.

MR. SNAP. I, sir? I, sir! Be more careful, sir.

CARTWRIGHT. Which is my room, Mr. Snap?

MR. SNAP. I will show you. 'Tis in the best of taste. I furnished it myself. *(They exit* L. *And as they do so,* CARTWRIGHT *in the lead,* WILD, *a burly, boisterous man of forty, enters* C.*)* Ah! Mr. Wild.

JONATHAN. My locket—my silver locket— Have they seized that villain Fierce?

MR. SNAP. We've just jailed him.

JONATHAN. Well, speed his trial, for if they hang me before they hang him, I'll never collect my bounty.

MR. SNAP. Then I'll collect it for you— (MR. SNAP *exits* R. JONATHAN *looks on table* L.C. *for locket—goes to chimney and peers up it.* LA RUSE, *a polished, cynical, middle-aged man, enters* C.; *watches* JONATHAN *in amusement; takes snuff.)*

LA RUSE. You have missed something, Jonathan?

JONATHAN. My locket's gone.

LA RUSE. You are irritated, what! You should

use snuff—there is nothing so good for an irritation as snuff.

JONATHAN. *(Crossing to table* L.C.*)* Damn your snuff, sir! You know how I hate it. The thing is not here—it is not to be found—'tis incomprehensible. *(Sits at table, searching.)*

LA RUSE. You have the fault of all great men— you permit yourself to be absorbed by a single business. Yes, greatness is narrowness, preoccupation; second rate men like myself must take refuge in the variation of clouds, images, women.

JONATHAN. A pox on your women! I am sure I made an entry of it.

LA RUSE. *(Looking into the sky; dreamily)* There are birds in the air, Jonathan, white birds! They are crying something to me which I do not understand. *(Affects to listen to the birds)* What are you telling me—you free things? *(He is joyful)* You are crying, one of your kind will soon fly to me—with wings for myself! Wings—wings to bear me far away! Yes, yes. It will be a bird who nests in the sun—a white bird! *(Suddenly)* What? It will not be a white bird? *(He becomes sorrowful)* It will be a black bird. *(He shivers)* My wings will be black.

JONATHAN. *(Convulsively)* A thousand hells! La Ruse! This is no time for your coloured words.

LA RUSE. Your obedient servant, Jonathan.

JONATHAN. *(Striking the table for emphasis)* Mr. Fierce, sir, is dishonest.

LA RUSE. This is appalling. You are sure?

JONATHAN. Mr. Fierce had scarcely brought me the locket—I had scarcely entered it on my records, when I missed it again.

LA RUSE. But pray, why should he bring you the locket and then take it away again?

JONATHAN. Because he knew he wouldn't have lived long if he hadn't apparently given it to me. La Ruse, do you know what the rogue did further?

While I had left the room for a few moments he obliterated the records, wiped it from my books. I did not credit him with so much wit.

LA RUSE. We have been fooled, then, by a damnable sharper, what! By my honour, I'll call him out— I'll run him through with dispatch— *(Away a little.)*

JONATHAN. *(Rises)* My dear Count, long before I missed the locket I swore out a warrant against Mr. Fierce.

LA RUSE. A warrant?

JONATHAN. 'Tis the principle of the thing!

LA RUSE. You have delivered him to the hangman?

JONATHAN. Candidly, my dear Count, I thought my delivering him up might favorably affect my fate.

LA RUSE. *(Bowing)* To me you will always be the great Jonathan, whatever your fate.

JONATHAN. You've heard? They've set the date for my hanging?

LA RUSE. No.

JONATHAN. Bah. What is it to be hanged? 'Tis but a dance—without music. *(Sits on table.)*

LA RUSE. They'll never hang you, Jonathan.

JONATHAN. Yet consider my position, La Ruse. Why should I hang when the Prime Minister is spared? He is the leader of a party, I am the leader of a gang; but both are primarily organized for spoils. And I am to be hanged, not because I differ from those who make and maintain the Law, but because I am too much like them for their own liking. It is declared that I have sacrificed my tools! Can you name me the statesman who has sacrificed his career for a friend? Then why am I to be garroted—rather than received at Court? Because, my fallen aristocratic friend, I was not born an aristocrat. But whatever my fate, your rotten aristocracy will not long survive me. The future belongs to men like myself—self-made men, if I may coin a phrase —the powers of government will yet pass into the hands of men who know how to build an organization, and make it profitable.

LA RUSE. Yes, yes, you are concentrated; we are diverted. A stray tune—a pretty face— a lyrical line, illusions us. You are not illusioned. Life— *(Up stage.* JONATHAN *crosses* R.*)*

MR. SNAP. *(Enters* L.*)* Life! Did you say life, Count? And what could be better than life on such a morning? The air! The balmy air! What! You haven't been out in the balmy air?

LA RUSE. Our spirits have wandered abroad, sir. *(Crosses down* L.*)*

MR. SNAP. Spirits indeed! Did you say spirits? They've no lungs, sir—you must have lungs for the enjoyment of the air! Why, the streets are packed with knaves. What could have kept you here on such a fragrant morning, gentlemen?

JONATHAN. Do not answer him, Count. He but mocks us. *(Sits* R.C.*)*

MR. SNAP. Come, sir, let the Count answer for himself.

LA RUSE. *(At top chair)* You are easily answered. Our spirits have wandered abroad, but our bodies, detained by locks, bolts, bars and judicial process, have necessarily languished where you see them now.

MR. SNAP. Spoken like a scholar, sir. I vow 'tis the very essence of an education to keep you jailed by me. You must pardon my little joke at your expense, but I am in high spirits. I have just jailed a poet.

JONATHAN. Truth to tell, Mr. Snap, I thought your joke in exceeding bad taste—twitting us with our lack of liberty.

MR. SNAP. *(Visibly incensed)* Bad taste! Did you

say bad taste? What! Shall the taste of a jailer be questioned by his felons? What! I am not to have my little joke—simply because you are condemned?

JONATHAN. *(Starting—ashen-faced)* You have heard—they've set the date for my hanging?

MR. SNAP. I have heard nothing. You have set me out of temper with your impertinence, sir! I am no longer in high spirits. I am in exceeding low spirits—and your fault, Mr. Wild. (JONATHAN *finds the world too much for him.)* What! Does he sniffle!

LA RUSE. He has had a troublous morning, Mr. Snap. *(Sympathetically)* Jonathan, pray retire to your room.

MR. SNAP. Does he forget that it is only by my grace that he continues to carry on his nefarious business, in jail, as out?

LA RUSE. You accept a certain percentage of the transactions, I believe.

MR. SNAP. I do, I do, and I won't deny it for my soul's sake—except under oath.

LA RUSE. I honour you for owning you are not squeamish, Mr. Snap.

MR. SNAP. I will tell you what, Sir Fop; I am not squeamish—there's not a man in London will say I am squeamish—distinctly, I am not! But as for your friend here—I am squeamish. What! Weeping! Sensitive! This father of bridle-culls—mill-kens—buttocks-and-files—assassins! (JONATHAN *groans.)* This thieving pimp and pimping thief! This fence —who has taught men to steal and then delivered 'em up for the bloody bounty? You may lay to what I have said, sir, as Jack Ketch will presently lay to Mr. Wild.

LA RUSE. *(Smiling; taking snuff)* You are a gentleman, Mr. Snap—

MR. SNAP. *(Thumpingly)* I am obliged to you for the notification, sir.

JONATHAN. *(Leaping to his feet and striding L.)* Sir, as you can see, I can scarcely articulate— I am distraught—a wronged man—but your words shall not go unanswered—my spirit cries out in rebuttal! You are a fool, Mr. Snap—you pervert the truth of my life—which a man of your mean stature must misunderstand. Know, then, sir, that I have an awkward pride in my nature, which is better pleased with being at the head of the lowest class than at the bottom of the highest. *(He pauses for breath. COUNT LA RUSE lays his snuff-box on the table and places a strengthening hand on his friend's shoulder.)* Permit me to say, though the idea may be somewhat coarse, I had rather stand on the summit of a dung-hill than at the bottom of a hill in Paradise! *(He collapses into chair L. of L.C. table.)*

LA RUSE. Your words, Jonathan, are like those pebbles which in the mouth of another Demosthenes turned into jewels. *(JONATHAN'S anguished fingers happen on the snuff-box.)* Ah, Mr. Snap, you do not understand Mr. Wild. *(JONATHAN pinches snuff-box.)* I, Count La Ruse, an exile from my country, a stranger in your country, alone understand his true greatness. *(The snuff-box disappears up JONATHAN'S capacious sleeve.)*

JONATHAN. *(Rising unsteadily)* Alone—alone—I ask only to be alone. *(He makes for the R. door)* 'Tis the principle of the thing—

MR. SNAP. *(Rushing between him and the exit)* Hold! Do you dare complain?

JONATHAN. *(Piteously)* Let me leave, Mr. Snap. I have every reason to leave immediately.

LA RUSE. Mr. Wild complains of nothing—but that you stand between him and the door.

MR. SNAP. *(Whirling on him)* Complain, sir! Do you not both eat at my table?

LA RUSE. A man of my position honours your table, Mr. Snap. But do not let us quarrel. Let me admit that I will never forget the way you have treated me—never. *(Crosses up stage a little; works round* R.*)*

MR. SNAP. That's a better tune than you have been singing, sir.

JONATHAN. *(Darting by him)* Alone—alone—all things conspire against me. *(He exits* L.*)*

MR. SNAP. *(Grumbling)* Ay, twelve good men and true have conspired to hang him by the neck— *(*JONATHAN *slams door.)* until dead. Bad taste, indeed! *(To* C.*)* What do you do at the door, sir?

LA RUSE. *(Shuts door)* A keyhole is like a woman, Mr. Snap; it tells secrets to the world. *(He goes to the fireplace, reaches up the flue and finds something there; he gives it to* MR. SNAP*)* Mr. Wild's silver locket as I promised. He blames its loss on the unfortunate Fierce.

MR. SNAP. *(Examining it with delight)* Sound, shining silver. By everything holy, a valuable ornament for some fat Duke's slim mistress. *(Crosses slightly* R.*)*

LA RUSE. *(Watching* MR. SNAP's *avarice with a peculiar disdain)* I doubt not such will be its fate. Beauty the world over is born in silence, and dies in carnival.

MR. SNAP. We shall profit by this, never fear. I have yet to see a more desirable trinket.

LA RUSE. I hold there are still more desirable trinkets to be had, sir.

MR. SNAP. *(Reverently)* And if you can't lay your hands on them, there's no thief in London can.

LA RUSE. Thank you, Mr. Snap. Nothing's so pleasing to the ear of man as flattery. But the things to which I had reference have no pawnable subtance—they lie safely hidden in the silver locket of the spirit.

MR. SNAP. Well, I suppose you must talk so. But it puzzles me why so many of the gentry should be of a melancholic frame of mind. They seem to drink bitterness from their mother's rich breasts. *(Crosses down* R. LAETITIA *appears in the* C. *door. She is twenty-nine, a ravishing woman; vital to the excess of carnality.)* Good morning, daughter. 'Tis Laetitia, Count.

LA RUSE. *(With an elaborate gesture)* The enchanting Mistress Laetitia. *(Down* L. *of table.)*

LAETITIA. *(With one of her own)* The noble Count Ruse.

MR. SNAP. Daughter, I have business. *(To door* R.*)* You must cheer the Count— Aye, cheer him, but not to the point where you might lose your maidenly reserve— I would not have that. *(He goes, with a final admonition of his head.)*

LAETITIA. *(Laughs—throws her arms wide)* Take me, La Ruse.

LA RUSE. *(Studying the manufacture of a chair)* I am not in a mood.

LAETITIA. *(Undiscomfited)* I adore you, La Ruse. I do. Show me the lover who knows how to renounce me—ay, and how to denounce me—and he shall be surfeited with my fidelity.

LA RUSE. Liar!

LAETITIA. *(Approaching him)* I am mad about you, La Ruse. Are you not mad about me?

LA RUSE. I abominate you.

LAETITIA. And yet you make love to me.

LA RUSE. Because I abominate you.

LAETITIA. 'Tis your one drawback as a lover that your reasoning is always original.

LA RUSE. And true. The surrender of a woman one adores is but tepid compared to the subjection of a woman one abominates. Therefore— *(He clasps and kisses her.)*

LAETITIA. *(Sparkling)* For a prisoner, sir, you take more liberties than a free man dares.

LA RUSE. *(Coldly, leaving her)* Pray remember,

Madam, you have granted me greater liberties than any I now implore.

LAETITIA. It is the privilege of a lady to remember, sir, as it is the duty of a gentleman to forget. (LA RUSE *sits* R. *of table.*) But alas! When a gentleman becomes a lover, he ceases to be a gentleman; the one is killed in the other. Yet I adore you, La Ruse, and would not willingly be without you.

LA RUSE. I shall be free of you yet.

LAETITIA. I shall do my best to hold you here. Yet you are foolish, sir—imagining you can escape me merely by leaving me.

LA RUSE. Out of this jail, and I am out of your life.

LAETITIA. Leave these prison walls, and your days shall still be spent in matching your mind against my mind—your nights, *(Sits on his knee)* in matching your strength against my strength—your time, always, in matching your malice against my malice. *(Kisses him)* You desire me, La Ruse.

LA RUSE. I desire no woman. I have found too many hairs—of too many colours—on my shoulder. *(Surveying her hair; critically)* Your own is far from the most attractive shade I have found on my shoulder.

LAETITIA. But it is the final shade you will find there. *(Rises)* You and I can no more escape from each other than from the reflection we must see if we look in the glass, or from the shadow we must see if we walk in the sun.

LA RUSE. But you forget—one may easily walk out of the sun. *(Rises; crosses* L., *above table.)*

LAETITIA. *(Lightly)* You will not kill yourself yet, La Ruse.

LA RUSE. *(Intensely)* Not while there is still a chance I may be free of you. But if the day should come—

LAETITIA. Egoist! Do you think yourself alone in

resenting the tie which binds us? Do you never think I have my own moods when I would be free of you?

LA RUSE. Would that they came more often!

LAETITIA. What if I should tell you—I had yielded to such a mood?

LA RUSE. I should be indifferent.

LAETITIA. I have yielded to such a mood.

LA RUSE. *(Instantly jealous)* You lie.

LAETITIA. No.

LA RUSE. Come here to me, hussy.

LAETITIA. *(Studying the manufacture of chair R. of table)* I am not in a mood. *(Crosses to chair.)*

LA RUSE. You are simply revengeful.

LAETITIA. And perhaps—I may yield to another such mood!

LA RUSE. Do so, and be damned.

LAETITIA. This is not indifference. This is love!

LA RUSE. Why? And what if it were proved anew what everyone knows: that a woman like yourself has many mouths—all of them lying? *(Sits on table.)*

LAETITIA. Does it mean something to you—that I have been lying?

LA RUSE. Yes. Is it not absurd? I cannot bear the thought of another embracing you with love, although I embrace you with loathing!

LAETITIA. Reassure yourself, La Ruse. I adore you. Yet, what if I had deceived you? 'Twould be no more on my part than the closing of my eyes in an amorous day-dream. The dream would pass quickly, my eyes would open—and your enduring image would be still in the glass before me.

LA RUSE. I am unworthy of such chaste fidelity. *(Rises)* But since you are so sure of me, why do you deny the favour I have petitioned a thousand times?

LAETITIA. *(Insolently)* To slip the great lock for you? Why should I?

LA RUSE. Because I go mad in my confinement here.

LAETITIA. *(Amazed. Crosses* L.*)* But, La Ruse, La Ruse! *(Sits* L. *of table)* 'Twas what you said to me when I first saw you in the jail! When I persuaded Papa to bring you here! This is ungracious of you, sir.

LA RUSE. I tell you, minx, I go mad here! Why will you not slip the lock for me? If all you have spoken is true, I shall still be yours while in full flight from you.

LAETITIA. But in an abstraction not wholly satisfactory to the warmth of my nature!

LA RUSE. What if I were to give you my word to return when I had paid the debt which sent me here?

LAETITIA. Poor Papa is fond of observing *(Rises)* you were well-born. Alas, Count La Ruse! We ladies who were not well-born have learned to our cost that the word of a gentleman is not always sacred when given to a lady of another class.

LA RUSE. You wrong yourself, Laetitia. You do belong to my class.

LAETITIA. *(Not without a trace of bitterness)* I am a jailer's wench—and past time I was married.

LA RUSE. No matter, you belong to my class: The devil has elevated you to his submerged party. You talk like no jailer's wench; you have been given an infernal gift of tongues. You act like no jailer's wench; you do as you please, and it is your present pleasure to torture me by holding me here.

LAETITIA. I have heard there is no happier state than to be the prisoner of love.

LA RUSE. There is no happier state—when one is the jailer. *(Crosses* R.*)*

LAETITIA. *(Clapping her hands)* Was ever a woman so forunate as myself—to have her lover under lock and key? I vow, sir, half the great love tragedies would have been comedies had the ladies been placed in my position. *(Crosses to c.)*

LA RUSE. This may yet prove more of a comedy than you think, Madam.

LAETITIA. You mean, La Ruse, that you have been tampering with the great lock.

LA RUSE. *(Casually)* Among others.

LAETITIA. Yes. You have also been tampering with the locks of Papa's arms-chest.

LA RUSE. Nothing is so easily beaten into shape of a key—as a pistol or knife.

LAETITIA. The locks are strong everywhere to hold you. *(Crosses to L. of table.)*

LA RUSE. *(Fiercely)* My spirit is strong everywhere to be free.

LAETITIA. Then our repulsions shall lend an intense piquance to our emotions. We shall spend delicious hours hating one another. You will visit me later, La Ruse?

LA RUSE. *(Studying the manufacture of R.C. chair)* I am not in a mood.

LAETITIA. *(Dangerously)* Take care, sir! There is always a refuge for a neglected woman! There is always— *(She is interrupted by the entrance of CART-WRIGHT, L.)*

CARTWRIGHT. *(Very much abashed)* I beg your pardon. I thought— *(He makes a motion to withdraw.)*

LAETITIA. *(Lyrically)* Stay, young gentleman! *(She flashes a mischievous glance at LA RUSE)* You are a stranger, sir? I do not remember seeing you.

CARTWRIGHT. I was taken only this morning. *(He feels that—somehow—he has spoken too freely, and again attempts to withdraw.)*

LAETITIA. *(Persuasively)* Do not run away, young gentleman. *(She repeats her mischievous glance at LA RUSE.)*

LA RUSE. *(Exploding)* Get out, you young fool.

(CARTWRIGHT'S *face darkens; he takes a step toward* LA RUSE.)

LAETITIA. *(Lays a restraining hand on the boy)* You must not mind Count La Ruse. He is not in a mood—or in a mood—I really forget which it is! Devote yourself rather to me.

CARTWRIGHT. I could not help but do that. I did not expect in such a place—

LAETITIA. Yes?

CARTWRIGHT. *(Colouring)* To find such loveliness.

LAETITIA. *(Delighted)* For shame, young gentleman! I vow not even the Count vies with you as a gallant.

CARTWRIGHT. *(Anxiously)* I would not have you think I was being merely a gallant. (LA RUSE *yawns—audibly.)*

LAETITIA. I would not think that, sir, for I hold there's no more pleasing charm than sincerity. *(Sits on table.* LA RUSE *yawns—audibly.)*

CARTWRIGHT. *(Looks at* LA RUSE*)* Though they are the fashion of the town, yet I despise these gallants—who make a mask of something better than a mask, a disguise of something real.

LA RUSE. *(Vigorously)* And I admire those gallants immensely, sir—because I am one myself. *(He goes closer to the couple)* I perceive from the nature of your eloquence you are hopelessly young.

LAETITIA. Divinely young, La Ruse.

CARTWRIGHT. *(Smarting at both references)* I was not arrested for the crime of youth, sir. *(Crossing front of chair* L. *of table.)*

LA RUSE. You should have been. At your age every man should be arrested and jailed until thirty. In this way, folly would be ended for all time.

CARTWRIGHT. *(Lashing back)* There is proverbially no fool like an old fool, sir.

LAETITIA. You mind Count La Ruse without

cause; he is by way of being a misanthrope; they say his mistress would be untrue to him.

LA RUSE. *(Sky-rocketing)* What is your name, sir?

CARTWRIGHT. *(Steps toward* LA RUSE*)* Mr. Cartwright.

LAETITIA. *(Applauding his tone. Rises)* I see you are as valiant as you are quick, Mr. Cartwright. But I pray you, gentlemen, for my sake—let your wits be your weapons.

CARTWRIGHT. Do you think I would fight him? I would not follow his code while I have courage to follow a better code: I have sworn never to lay my hands on a human being, except in love.

LAETITIA. *(Laughs)* Except in love?—You've been rude, La Ruse.

LA RUSE. *(Interested by the boy's naive declaration)* I meant no offense, sir. Last night's wine has left me on edge.

CARTWRIGHT. I regret the words passed. *(They bow to each other.)*

LAETITIA. *(Vastly entertained by the proceedings. Sits on table)* You were discussing the gallants, gentlemen; it promised to be most edifying to the ignorance of my female ears. *(Offers chair to* CARTWRIGHT.*)*

CARTWRIGHT. You were defending the beaux, Count La Ruse. *(Sits L. of table.)*

LA RUSE. Your servant, Mr. Cartwright. *(Crosses to chair R. of table)* I will prove my case. What is it, sir, to fall in love with a woman? 'Tis a most involuntary gesture; for a woman to be flattered when a man falls in love with her were as if she were to be flattered when a man catches the measles. He can no more help the one than the other. But gallantry, sir—gallantry is the deliberate wisdom of men who do choicely what fools must do willy-nilly;

and a woman of perception must always prefer your mature gentleman to your young idiot. I see that you take me amiss, Mr. Cartwright; you must permit me the license of a general remark. It follows, from what I have said, that the very spice of affectation is to appear more sincere than sincerity itself. I must blame my art when people think me insincere—because I so manifestly am.

CARTWRIGHT. *(Radically)* Count La Ruse: *(Rises; to above chair)* Your gallants have bravado, without bravery; courtesy, without sacrifice; honour, without a cause to die for.

LAETITIA. I vow, sir, but you talk beyond your years! You must be a collegian. *(Rises.)*

CARTWRIGHT. *(Proudly)* I was expelled.

LAETITIA. Expelled?

LA RUSE. 'Tis a special form of graduation, designed for the more original of the students.

CARTWRIGHT. *(With the same self-conscious defiance as when he admitted his talent to* MR. SNAP*)* I wrote a tract against God.

LAETITIA. That was wicked, sir. I am High Church, and devout. You look as if you were of good family, and sure, one of good family should not be atheistic.

CARTWRIGHT. *(The note of the born zealot kindling in his voice)* I am not atheistic. I believe in love.

LAETITIA. *(Excited)* We shall all be blasted! You are young; you have been led astray by books. You must let me convert you again. (LA RUSE *crosses* R.)

CARTWRIGHT. I must convert you.

LA RUSE. Would you leave me out in the wintry cold? What are the articles of your belief? *(Sits chair* R.C.*)*

CARTWRIGHT. *(With the full note of the zealot)* That the Paradise which men have lost is to be found again on earth. (LAETITIA *sits* R. *of table.)*

Is the air given us, only that we may stifle? Is the
sea given us, only that we may drown? Are the
flowers given us, only that we may faint? No. While
we dream of a distant Heaven, Heaven is at hand
for us to storm. I believe everything is forbidden by
men, yet the wise are passionate; that nothing is forbidden by nature, yet the wise are austere. I believe
that fear adds only to fear, hate adds only to hate,
but that beauty—beauty adds to everything. *(He has
been looking at* LAETITIA*)* And you— *(To her)* you
who are so radiant in my eyes, I believe you will
take my hand, you will walk with me into shadowy,
holy places.

LAETITIA. I know not whether to be flattered—or
frightened—or attracted by your presumption! Your
talk is strange.

CARTWRIGHT. Truth is strange.

LA RUSE. *(Extends his hand in the ancient Roman
salute)* Hail, Pilate!

LAETITIA. *(Rises; crosses to* C.*)* Why do you talk
so? Are you a poet?

CARTWRIGHT. Yes.

LAETITIA. Why did you not say as much before?
(To up C.*)* 'Tis in his nature, then—such incoher-
ence! *(Recovers her coquetry; as if thrilled)* A
poet! But how charming!

LA RUSE. I am not surprised to find you jailed;
the law and the muses have ever played ill together.
They are like Mistress Laetitia's spinet—out of
tune, the music jars.

LAETITIA. *(Winningly)* And will you write a
poem to me, Mr. Cartwright? Will you dedicate a
poem to me?

CARWRIGHT. My heart is doing so now.

LAETITIA. *(Away a little)* La Ruse, the pattern of
your conceits was never so taking as this. *(Up to
sofa.)*

LA RUSE. *(Bitingly)* Romantic vein! The inspiration of your muse is Mistress Laetitia, daughter of your jailer.

CARTWRIGHT. You are Mr. Snap's daughter?

LAETITIA. Do you hate me, now—since my father is your jailer?

CARTWRIGHT. You have set me free.

LA RUSE. *(Agonized)* Free! *(Rises)* Free! Never blaspheme with that word, sir.

CARTWRIGHT. I did not use it as a word, but as a mystery.

LA RUSE. *(Roughly)* You have another mystery to explain—your bursting in here without a by-your-leave.

CARTWRIGHT. I meant no disrespect. Mr. Snap has sold me the privacy of this floor.

LA RUSE. *(Warmly)* Oh! Indeed, Mr. Snap has sold me the privacy of this floor. 'Tis not the first time— *(The CLOCK strikes twelve.)*

LAETITIA. Noon! I must look to the cook; we shall be at table directly. I shall persuade Papa to let you sit at table with us, Mr. Cartwright.

CARTWRIGHT. You make me very happy, Mistress Laetitia. *(Bows.)*

LAETITIA. You shall sit by my side.

LA RUSE. *(As she passes, aside)* Minx!

CARTWRIGHT. You make me very happy!

LAETITIA. 'Twill be my aim to make you happier while you are lodged here. I must acquaint you afterwards with the more intimate ways of the place. *(Smiles enigmatically at LA RUSE, ravishingly at the poet, and exits C.)*

LA RUSE. *(Sits on sofa. Oblivious of CART-WRIGHT's enchantment)* I must ask you never to degrade the name of freedom by uttering it before that woman—before any woman. Yes, you will find monarchies are ruled by women, republics by men: for liberty bears a fiercer cut than Fashion permits.

Mr. Cartwright—I grieve to note you have heard not one of my priceless words.

CARTWRIGHT. I beg your pardon.

LA RUSE. You have heard the sirens' song, and are lost. How old are you, sir?

CARTWRIGHT. Twenty-one.

LA RUSE. Twenty-one! Are people still twenty-one? For what are you held?

CARTWRIGHT. For a debt of two hundred pounds.

LA RUSE. Odd! I am held for the precise amount.

CARTWRIGHT. How long have you been held?

LA RUSE. I was taken the year of the flood. Do you know, I have gambled away as much as fifty thousand pounds at a sitting; I have thrice been held for murder, each time justly—and each time been released within the week; and yet for a beggarly two hundred pounds I have been caged here these three long years?

CARTWRIGHT. *(Envisioning a like fate)* Three years!

LA RUSE. Two in the jail, and one here. Have you hope for a speedier release?

CARTWRIGHT. None.

LA RUSE. No parents?

CARTWRIGHT. I have an uncle.

LA RUSEE. Won't he help you?

CARTWRIGHT. He sent me here.

LA RUSE. You may console yourself with the thought that the malice of a relative is still more endurable than his affection. You borrowed from your uncle?

CARTWRIGHT. No, he sued me for my inheritance.

LA RUSE. And you lost your suit. I myself have several times been defended by eminent counsel, and each time been eminently convicted; for the fame of lawyers appears founded on the number of cases they lose, famously.

CARTWRIGHT. I won my suit.

LA RUSE. My rhetoric has gone astray. Then why are you here?

CARTWRIGHT. My lawyers had me arrested—perceiving as they did that I owed them more than the value of the property—which they seized.

LA RUSE. It is not the meek who will inherit the earth: it is the lawyers. Such is the testament of Count La Ruse. *(Rises.)*

CARTWRIGHT. Manifestly, you adopted that as a nom de plume.

LA RUSE. Say rather as a nom de crime. I was born—but no matter. The blood of kings flows in my veins.

CARTWRIGHT. *(With pride)* And in mine.

LA RUSE. The Homeric strain: a noble lineage. Beware, sir, lest you cross it with the treason of another Helen.

CARTWRIGHT. *(Resentfully)* Mistress Laetitia?

LA RUSE. You are acute. Yes, I meant Mistress Laetitia. But did I? *(Crosses R.)* Who knows what anyone means any more? The world threatens to be a garment which has gone out of style, while I still must wear it. This is death, to me, for I long ago took a sense of pleasure in place of my soul. *(Sits chair R.C.)*

CARTWRIGHT. I am sorry for you, Count La Ruse.

LA RUSE. Damn your impudence! Keep your sorrow for yourself; you will need it, here. When you have been detained as long as I have been, you will learn there is only one reality, and a bitter one.

CARTWRIGHT. *(Crosses to LA RUSE)* There is another reality—and I think I have found it.

LA RUSE. *(Shrugs his shoulders)* After all, what would it avail you if you desired freedom as passionately as I do?

CARTWRIGHT. *(Hesitantly)* I should find a way.

LA RUSE. *(Skeptical. Laughs)* What way, sir?

CARTWRIGHT. *(Uncertain if he is being wise)*
This way. *(He reveals a knife. Rises.)*

LA RUSE. *(Snatches it from him)* A knife!

CARTWRIGHT. *(Sure he has not been wise)* I have
never carried a blade. A prisoner slipped it to me
when we were searched.

LA RUSE. *(Feeling the blade; with mounting excitement)* Keen—keen! But why am I surprised?
Liberty is keen. *(He radiates the knife in the light)*
Bright—bright! But why am I surprised? Freedom
is bright. *(His exaltation approaches ecstacy)* Mouth
about your women, you son of Homer! Will they
glitter like this? A knife—I have a knife—a knife!

CARTWRIGHT. Let me have the knife back. You
grow over-excited.

LA RUSE. Over-excited? You are a poet—and
have no more perception? *(Closes his eyes in rapture; runs his fingers over the sharp edge)* I am
calm and at peace with the world at last. Life—my
sense of pleasure returns to me; already I am walking the streets, frequenting the tables, dining tete-a-
tete with the King's mistress! What hour, think you,
will be best?

CARTWRIGHT. Best—

LA RUSE. Midnight—

CARTWRIGHT. For what?

LA RUSE. *(Impatiently)* Why, when we shall excellently cut the throat of Mr. Snap—seize his keys
—and escape.

CARTWRIGHT. Mr. Snap! Laetitia's father!

LA RUSE. *(Too engrossed by the future to notice
the poet's horror)* Hell's father, sir! *(He radiates
the blade again.)*

CARTWRIGHT. *(Snatches vainly)* The knife is
mine.

LA RUSE. Yours, sir? You are mistaken. The
blade has been in my family for generations, and

sentiment forbids me let it go. *(Puts knife in pocket.)*

CARTWRIGHT. *(Impotently)* I'll not be responsible for the cutting of any throats!

LA RUSE. *(Dismissing the subject)* You will never make a great poet, sir, for I see you are a moral man.

CARTWRIGHT. I will not harm Mistress Laetitia.

LA RUSE. *(Solemnly)* She will harm you—

CARTWRIGHT. You have some cause to be malicious.

LA RUSE. I will tell you, Mr. Cartwright: it would profit you more in Heaven to cut the throat of Mr. Snap—than to kiss the throat of his daughter.

CARTWRIGHT. Doubtless Mistress Laetitia has repelled your advances.

LA RUSE. *(Sadly)* There is only one possible explanation of this world, Mr. Cartwright: the Gods themselves are stupid. Yes. For that reason it is said we were made in their image. They have had one brilliant idea, sir: snuff. *(He feels for his snuff-box; finds it gone; recalls that he left it on the table, and looks there)* Gone! My snuff-box gone! Your precious Mr. Snap—or that other damnable rogue— *(Crosses to table.)*

CARTWRIGHT. Jonathan Wild?

LA RUSE. *(Searching frantically)* The identical villain! I would have parted with my bowels, before that box. It was given me by—a lady! You are new here, Mr. Cartwright; let me warn you against Mr. Wild—and Mr. Snap; two of the consummate thieves of the age. (CARTWRIGHT *crosses to table.)* 'Tis not to be found! Wild was here—Snap was here—is it possible that that minx—? 'Twas while Wild was here— I was comforting him. By God, I'll have it back or I'll demolish the house. *(Crosses to sofa, then down to chair* R.C. CARTWRIGHT *surveys the room. He sees some paper at table, sits back of*

*table and begins writing a lyric. He has scarcely
begun, however, when* LAETITIA *enters* C. CART-
WRIGHT *to chair* R. *of table.)*

LAETITIA. Oh, La Ruse! Pray, leave the house
stand at least for dinner, which is ready.

LA RUSE. Damn dinner! I couldn't digest nectar
at the moment!

LAETITIA. What's happened to him?

CARTWRIGHT. He's lost his snuff-box.

LAETITIA. What a pity. If he had it now he might
sneeze out his temper.

LA RUSE. If I had it now I wouldn't be in a temper.

LAETITIA. 'Tis the oddest matter, (LA RUSE *looks
round sofa.)* but one is forever losing things in this
charming house.

CARTWRIGHT. For myself I have found much
more here than I could ever lose—

LAETITIA. I vow, Mr. Cartwright, you are a sweet
young man.

LA RUSE. When you hear that purring—look out
for claws, Mr. Cartwright.

LAETITIA. You're in need of food. (WILD *appears*
L.) Ah! Mr. Wild— Dinner waits—

LA RUSE. *(Glares at* WILD) Let it wait, Madam.
I've been robbed of my appetite by the scoundrel
who robbed me of my snuff-box—a treasured piece
of mine.

JONATHAN. Sir, you look palpably at me when
you say that! Sir, do you dare imply—

LA RUSE. Sir, I imply I want my snuff-box back
at once!

LAETITIA. *(Nervously)* Stand aside from them,
Mr. Cartwright.

JONATHAN. Sir, I'll not have you talk to me in
this manner; 'tis the principle of the thing! *(Coolly)*
Yes. As a principled man, have I asked you for the
return of my silver locket?

LA RUSE. *(To* JONATHAN*)* Do you dare imply—
(WARN Curtain.)

LAETITIA. *(Firmly)* Enough. We shall have no more of your joint ill-manners! La Ruse, you must look for your box later—and you, Mr. Wild, for your locket. *(Turns up stage.)*

LA RUSE. *(Fuming)* By Heaven, Madam, you may depend that I will! *(Crosses to sofa.)*

MR. SNAP. *(Bustles in* R.*)* I am in high spirits again; they bubble over.

LAETITIA. Stop your nonsense, Papa, and come along. *(She takes the poet by the arm)* I'll show you, as we pass, how the rooms lie, sir. *(Notices* LA RUSE*)* Come along, La Ruse.

LA RUSE. *(Vaguely; to himself)* White birds—

LAETITIA. Awaken La Ruse, Papa. *(Goes out* C. *with* CARTWRIGHT.*)*

MR. SNAP. Come along, Count. *(Crosses to* C. WILD *disappears off* C.*)* Wild hangs tomorrow. *(Chuckles.)*

LA RUSE. Tomorrow? You say Wild hangs tomorrow?

LAETITIA'S VOICE. *(Vexed)* Come along, Papa.

MR. SNAP. Coming, Daughter. You are ready, Count? *(Turns toward the* C. *door.)*

LA RUSE. *(Looks at the knife behind* MR. SNAP's *back)* Quite ready, dear Mr. Snap.

CURTAIN

ACT TWO

The same, that night. The room is lighted by an adequate number of candles; the window remains open. The papers, etc., have been removed from the table.

LA RUSE *discovered on sofa, looking out of window at rise.*

MR. SNAP. *(Enters c.)* Ah! La Ruse, I'm belching affluently. *(Crosses to table R. of table L.C.)*

LA RUSE. That was a most excellent supper, Mr. Snap. *(Musing)* I believe I shall never sup better in your house—never.

MR. SNAP. *(Sardonic)* Did you say never? You are not thinking of trying to leave us through your window again, Count?

LA RUSE. No. This time I shall leave through your front door. When the clock strikes twelve I shall vanish like the maid with the glass slipper.

MR. SNAP. *(Pleasantly entertained)* And if you do, sir, Cinderella'll find a coach awaiting her at the door—a police-coach! I am delighted, Count. *(Sits R. of table L.C.)* You have recovered your good humour.

LA RUSE. I protest, Mr. Snap. *(Crosses to chair back of table L.C.)* You never saw me in better humour than today at noon.

MR. SNAP. You'll not deny you grew sulky during afternoon.

LA RUSE. I was bored. I was resentful at being left alone.

MR. SNAP. It was plain to see you were in a rage against yourself.

LA RUSE. *(With sudden vehemence)* Not against myself.

MR. SNAP. *(Always prepared to take umbrage)* Against me, sir? Against me? Had you the audacity to resent me at my own table?

LA RUSE. *(His anger dying away in soul-weariness)* Not against you, Mr. Snap.

MR. SNAP. Then against who—or what, sir?

LA RUSE. Who can tell? *(Sits in chair)* One has memories, Mr. Snap—or better, one has not. Perhaps I was in a rage against the sun which rises. Perhaps against my first love—or my last. Strange, that one should forget one's last love before one's first!

MR. SNAP. By the bye, while you were vexed with Laetitia's absence this afternoon then, she was in her room.

LA RUSE. Yes. Did you notice Mr. Cartwright at supper? He was singularly animated.

MR. SNAP. He is odd, sir, like all of his kind. He spent the afternoon in his room with his metrical ruminations.

LA RUSE. Yes, I had thundered on his door, without arousing him.

MR. SNAP. Pray, Count, you have said naught of Mr. Wild and his fate.

LA RUSE. You've not told him he hangs tomorrow?

MR. SNAP. *(Considerate)* It seemed a pity to spoil his supper.

LA RUSE. *(Unforgiving)* Damn him. He has spoiled my after-supper.

MR. SNAP. *(Craftily)* I have been thinking of

telling him—but I have been thinking more of not telling him.

LA RUSE. *(Pricks up his ears)* How now? What is in your agile mind?

MR. SNAP. Mr. Wild is a man of wealth.

LA RUSE. *(With conviction)* He is certainly the possessor of a valuable snuff-box.

MR. SNAP. He has money.

LA RUSE. Everybody's money.

MR. SNAP. He is about to die.

LA RUSE. Has he relatives?

MR. SNAP. Relatives? Did you say relatives? He has seven wives.

LA RUSE. What do you propose?

MR. SNAP. What if we tell him that a reprieve is possible—if he acts wisely and quickly?

LA RUSE. You would delude him into the belief he could be saved—when he must surely hang in the morning?

MR. SNAP. *(His little eyes dancing)* 'Tis the very point, that. He will be on his way to the gallows ere he's aware of his duping! 'Twill be choking late then for a hue and a cry over what money we get from him!

LA RUSE. Mr. Snap, forgive me. *(Rises)* I had failed to perceive the sublime heights of your imag-:ination.

MR. SNAP. *(Beams)* I'll admit, I think the plot neatly contrived.

LA RUSE. Yes, but why only a reprieve? Why not a full pardon—

MR. SNAP. For that we can easily garner a hundred pounds from the unfeeling villain!

LA RUSE. One hundred pounds. That's but fifty for each of us! Why not more, Mr. Snap?

MR. SNAP. Why, we cannot gouge him of more; he would not pay more, not for his very life, sir!

LA RUSE. *(Soliloquises)* The plot is neat— Jonathan is close, he parts unwilling from a bad farthing, but he fears death—how he fears death! *(Sits)* Mr. Snap, do you fear death?

MR. SNAP. *(Upset)* Death? Did you say death? 'Tis a word as chilling as a cold sheet.

LA RUSE. There may always be a hot brick for your feet, Mr. Snap.

MR. SNAP. Do not say death, sir! I've no use for the word—no use at all!

LA RUSE. *(Encouragingly)* You are in good health, Mr. Snap.

MR. SNAP. *(Brightens)* I've never a day of sickness.

LA RUSE. *(Thoughtfully)* And still, you can never be sure. Health is no sign we shall not die. Death comes like a thief in the night—like a stab in the dark. Yes, I hear a beating of dark wings, now.

MR. SNAP. *(Terrified)* If you continue to rave on, I'll leave you! 'Tis my heart you hear beating; you have set shivers like lice running down my spine. Were the wind to blow a candle out, I'd think my life blown out!

LA RUSE. *(Blows out a candle)* There, sir, 'tis the candle's flame gone out, not yours! *(Rises; lights candle at fireplace.)*

MR. SNAP. *(Rises)* Be done with your cursed fancies—done, I say!

LA RUSE. *(Asquiesces)* Think you he could procure the money tonight? *(Crosses to SNAP.)*

MR. SNAP. I don't know. I've tapped the walls of his room, sounded the floor and all to no effect, yet I could swear he must have coin o' the realm where he could lay his hand on't.

LA RUSE. But why not bell the cat yourself and keep all the profits?

MR. SNAP. I am not enough of an actor for the role, sir. Mr. Wild, being a knave, would see through to my native honesty. (LAETITIA *sings and plays spinet off stage.)* Now, with your refined ability— *(Crosses to door* L. *VOICES are heard, passing through the hall.)*

LA RUSE. *(Listens; becomes intense)* 'Tis Laetitia and her poet. *(The VOICES are heard in the adjoining room.)*

MR. SNAP. Call him now!

LA RUSE. *(Looks gloomily toward the voices)* No, later. I have somewhat to say to Laetitia. *(Crosses up to* C.*)*

MR. SNAP. *(Authoritative)* No, no, 'tis not Laetitia hangs tomorrow. We must first dispose of Mr. Wild. *(Calling)* Mr. Wild! Mr. Wild!

JONATHAN. *(Heard off stage)* Yes, Mr. Snap.

MR. SNAP. He's coming— *(Crosses to door* R.*)* Remember, one hundred pounds.

JONATHAN. *(Enters* L.*)* Yes, Mr. Snap.

MR. SNAP. *(As he exits* R.*)* Count La Ruse has something to say to you, Mr. Wild. *(Exits.)*

JONATHAN. You are disturbed, La Ruse: pray, why? *(Sits* L. *of table.)*

LA RUSE. I am disturbed, sir: I'll not permit myself to be disturbed. What! Shall the stars be obscured by a slut? *(Crosses to door* R.*)*

JONATHAN. I sympathize with your tender emotion, Count.

LA RUSE. Jonathan! Mr. Snap has asked me to speak to you for him—to give you good news!

JONATHAN. *(Gasps)* I am not to hang?

LA RUSE. Not quite.

JONATHAN. How, not quite? They will hang me a few feet lower? There's something uncommon in this, La Ruse. Why should you speak for Mr. Snap?

LA RUSE. Mr. Snap feared his inflammable nature —feared that with the best of wills you would come to words again.

JONATHAN. 'Tis still no reason he should not speak for himself.

LA RUSE. *(Sits R. of table)* You are right, Jonathan. 'Tis but the reason he gave me. He asked me to speak, because he knew me to be your loyal friend —but mostly because he fears to be seen in what must remain, after all, a hanging matter.

JONATHAN. Fears to be seen! Your reasoning grows sounder; Mr. Snap is not the soul of courage.

LA RUSE. *(Grows animated)* Courage, Jonathan? You have not heard the extent of his cowardice. Not only will he not speak—he'll not accept your money himself! No, sir! It must be passed him through me.

JONATHAN. *(Upset)* Money? Money for what?

LA RUSE. You know Mr. Snap.

JONATHAN. I know Mr. Snap.

LA RUSE. He has been feeling his way—

JONATHAN. In my room. I have watched him through a crack. There's not a board hasn't felt the soft caress of his fingers.

LA RUSE. Nevertheless, Mr. Snap has been feeling his way towards a full pardon for you, Jonathan. I see you do not believe it.

JONATHAN. Pity is not in Mr. Snap's nature as in yours or mine, Count.

LA RUSE. You forget there are moments when even pity may be combined with profit.

JONATHAN. There's truth in that: it had not struck me before. Mr. Snap would not willingly lose my board, for I am vilely over-charged. There's no tavern in London charges what Mr. Snap charges me for the privilege of being speeded forth some morning on a terrible journey. Though I feign otherwise, Count, I dread that journey of all things.

LA RUSE. You will never make that journey, Jonathan, if you listen well. Of all people, you should be aware that men in office are—men in office.

JONATHAN. Well—to the terms. What am I asked to slip from the halter?

LA RUSE. *(Dismissing it as a bagatelle)* Three hundred pounds.

JONATHAN. *(Appalled)* Three hundred pounds!

LA RUSE. There are many to be bribed. If you pay me the money, you may believe me, Mr. Snap will see but little of it. (LAETITIA *is heard singing and playing spinet off stage.)*

JONATHAN. I'll not pay it! What! Pay three hundred pounds to a set of rogues who should be in my place? Let them do it—let it come! By Heaven, they'll not have three hundred pounds from me— not for my life! 'Tis not worth it—

LA RUSE. *(Shrugs his shoulders)* For myself, I should think a thousand pounds cheap. 'Tis likely, as you choke, you'll wish you'd not been so covetous. *(Turns up stage.)*

JONATHAN. Covetous, sir? 'Tis the principle of the thing!—What shall I do? *(Hopefully)* They'll take less.

LA RUSE. *(Decisively)* No. Your reprieve will bring a clamour on their—*(MUSIC stops.)*—heads. You must let them have a fat umbrella for the storm. 'Tis three hundred pounds or your life.

JONATHAN. *(Groans)* My money or my life! How do I know, sir, if I pay this money I'll get the pardon?

LA RUSE. You must take the chance, Jonathan. I am convinced the offer is authentic. Mr. Snap is not enough of an actor to have deceived me.

JONATHAN. Very well—I'll pay—but after the pardon is signed.

LA RUSE. Do you think you deal with infants, sir? Why, they have made it a point the money be delivered at once—tonight.

JONATHAN. *(His suspicions re-awakened)* Tonight? Why so quickly?

LA RUSE. You force me to be unsparing, Jonathan. Those in power say you are such a monstrous villain they are not anxious to do't, not even for the money. You must pin them down at once.

JONATHAN. Three hundred pounds! (LAETITIA *and* CARTWRIGHT *are heard laughing off stage.*) 'Tis Laetitia and Cartwright. They're coming.

LA RUSE. *(Rising)* Damn Laetitia. I never want to see her again as long as I live. But by God I'll see her once before the night is over when I'm through with you, Mr. Wild— *(They exit* L. LAETITIA *opens the* C. *door and enters with* CARTWRIGHT. *She carries an elegant fan, which she uses well.)*

LAETITIA. *(With a shade of disappointment)* I thought I heard voices. (CARTWRIGHT *kisses her.)* La Ruse usually repairs here *(Crosses to light lamps)* at this time.

CARTWRIGHT. We are fortunate, then.

LAETITIA. Yes, we are fortunate. *(Crosses; lights candles. They cross to the sofa.)* 'Tis more pleasant in this room. Let us sit by the window. *(Taps him with her fan)* The night is warm for the spring. *(Sits on sofa.)*

CARTWRIGHT. I could not keep my eyes from you, at table. *(Crosses round sofa to her)* I wished only we were alone together in your room again.

LAETITIA. I noticed you, sir.

CARTWRIGHT. Why would you not meet my glance?

LAETITIA. You were injudicious enough.

CARTWRIGHT. Can love be injudicious?

LAETITIA. Can love be anything else?

CARTWRIGHT. I have had a dream—a dream of spring-madness!

LAETITIA. Madness sufficient to set up a flock of hatters shops! We were strangers this morning.

CARTWRIGHT. And now—*(Sits on sofa)*—we are not strangers.

LAETITIA. A single day has sufficed to change the years. I had always known it would be thus—when love at last came into my life—when at last I permitted the sweet and dangerous intimacy of a man! Comfort me, sir, with the assurance I have not yielded to one who took me lightly; let me hear you say, I love you.

CARTWRIGHT. I love you.

LAETITIA. I would believe you did I not know there are three things a man says with equal ease: "I love you—" "I regret, Madam, I can see you no more—" "By Gad, sir, she was as pretty a wench as ever I bedded!"

CARTWRIGHT. I love you! *(Kisses hand. Kneels.)*

LAETITIA. My naive heart would believe you—

CARTWRIGHT. Did I not tell you, this afternoon, I had saved myself for you—as you had saved yourself for me! I was waiting—waiting for someone who would share with me the immense burden of being. Often it seemed to me I was a fool. Spring came tenderly everywhere—so tenderly. Only to me it came like a sword. Laetitia, Laetitia, you have healed my wound of spring! My wound of life!

LAETITIA. I believe that you love me. And you must believe that I love you. *(Kiss)* Come, sir, let go of me—we shall be seen by the world. *(Rises.)*

CARTWRIGHT. The world will not like us? So much the worse for the world!

LAETITIA. So much the worse for us—nay, for me! Your arm—remove your arm, sir! *(Crosses L.C.)* My good name—'tis nothing to you?

CARTWRIGHT. *(Upset)* I meant no harm.

LAETITIA. No, only to hold me where we might be discovered! Alas, am I betrayed already? Is this the stuff of your oath, on the threshold of my room?

CARTWRIGHT. Forgive me.

LAETITIA. *(To him)* You will remember your promise. You will be discreet.

CARTWRIGHT. I will do always whatever you ask me. *(Away a little R.)*

LAETITIA. *(Relents further)* Come, sir, you have a face like Mr. Wild at the sight of a rope! My temper is out of me. *(Capriciously kisses him)* There, sir, you see! World or no world! *(Takes his hands. Kisses hand.)*

CARTWRIGHT. *(Lifted from the depths)* Laetitia! You are kind.

LAETITIA. *(Gaily. Lets go hand)* Now you are like Papa—in high spirits!

CARTWRIGHT. In Heaven!

LAETITIA. Where the cherubim sing, like the poets, always of the Spring? Tell me why poets must sing always of the Spring? *(Turns up C.)*

CARTWRIGHT. *(Carries the happy mood)* Because they are boys who must run to a fire. April's their fire. They stand too close and catch the flame.

LAETITIA. *(Sententious)* Wise children soon learn to stand away from the fire. *(Sits on table L.C.)*

CARTWRIGHT. *(Mystical)* Is it a part of wisdom— to stand away from the fire? *(Crosses to her.)*

LAETITIA. For all that, I do not like your Spring as I like my Autumn. The skies flame and meadows are cool, but your cool April love is crossed then by some hot wind sweeping back from summer, by an unseasonable heat burning life to a delicious decay. I could gallop, or swoon: the yellow on a leaf has curious power to make me desire. *(Laughs strangely and draws CARTWRIGHT close)* I must teach you the joy of things yellow-tinged, overripe, sir.

CARTWRIGHT. *(Impulsively)* Let me come to your room again tonight.

LAETITIA. It would be too dangerous. *(Crosses to C.)* I vow you will prove an eager lover. *(Restive, she walks here and there)* I must warn you, be neither too importunate nor too negligent; for one or t'other is the death of love— *(Crosses to chair R.C.)* I have read. *(Sits)* Where can La Ruse be, tonight?

CARTWRIGHT. *(Saddened)* I could almost believe you wished him with us. I dislike La Ruse.

LAETITIA. Would you be jealous of an impoverished rake? I have as little to do with him as possible—although I will confess he amuses me.

CARTWRIGHT. He is malicious. Why should he amuse you?

LAETITIA. Perhaps because he is malicious. Pray —there was something in your tone—has La Ruse warned you against me?

CARTWRIGHT. *(Hesitant)* Yes.

LAETITIA. *(Smiles)* It was like La Ruse. Truth to tell he made certain advances, and found me inaccessible.

CARTWRIGHT. *(Triumphant)* I guessed as much. *(Crosses to her a little)* And told him so.

LAETITIA. You shall have a kiss for that— *(He crosses to her.)* presently, Mr. Cartwright.

CARTWRIGHT. Must you still call me Mr. Cartwright? *(Away a little.)*

LAETITIA. More than ever, sir. *(Severely)* If our intimacy teaches you nothing else, let it teach you this—that discretion is the first talent of a lover. For the last time, I charge you to remember your promise to me— *(Rises)* Mr. Cartwright.

CARTWRIGHT. *(Subdued)* I will do always—

LAETITIA. Whatever I ask! Pray, how will you address me before others? Like this: Mistress Laetitia.

CARTWRIGHT. *(In her formal accents)* Mistress Laetitia. *(She crosses; sits on table* L.C. *With abrupt animation. He turns round)* But O! Vile and obscene! We must be formal: we must bow correctly for fear that our pure emotions will be weighed— checked—and found wanting, in the foul balance of the world! Young as I am, Laetitia, I believe love will redeem men when men have redeemed love. *(Up to her)* Dare with me, Laetitia! Let us cry of

the world we are true: we are lovers: our lips have
met: our bodies have burned with the clear fire of
our spirits: the sky is serene, the wind is tender,
because we are lovers! Let us heap flowers under a
white heaven on the green earth.

LAETITIA. *(Gasps)* 'Tis breath-taking to hear you
go on! 'Tis a parliamentary wind of words!

CARTWRIGHT. *(Obsessed)* Will you dare with me?

LAETITIA. Let me think awhile. Yes, 'tis a pretty
picture you have conjured for me! Two lovers, hand
in hand, walk desolate ways in defiance of the con-
ventions.

CARTWRIGHT. *(Prophetic: fierce)* Their desolation shall bloom.

LAETITIA. The fashionable world stands agape
and offended—but what of that? They have each
other. They are not received—but what of that?
They have each other. They are pilloried, they are
stoned—but what of that? They have each other. Always and always, each other.

CARTWRIGHT. *(Exalted)* And love, and victory.

LAETITIA. Always and always, each other. *(Starts
from her visionary posture; with sudden dismay)*
Yes—but what then?

CARTWRIGHT. *(Stupidly)* Then? When?

LAETITIA. *(In a torrent)* When they have had
each other for an eternity? When he tires of her
beauty and she of his oratory? When he cannot
abide her friends, and she deceives him with his
best friend? When, in short, they have had each
other to the point of wishing they had never had
each other?

CARTWRIGHT. *(Stricken)* You have been mocking
me.

LAETITIA. *(Sweetly)* I would not have you think
that. I was but measuring your ideal against the
reality of things. Come, sir. You must first convert
me, as you promised this morning.

CARTWRIGHT. *(Revived)* The grace of your spirit will make you understand.

LAETITIA. You shall have that promised kiss now. Tell me; how much do you love me?

CARTWRIGHT. *(Trembles)* Let me tell you in your room tonight.

LAETITIA. *(Agitated)* No, no— *(Rises; crosses up to sofa)* 'Twould be too dangerous! And yet—perhaps! Ask me again, sir. Not another word now! *(Sits on sofa)* I will see— (LA RUSE *enters* L. *She becomes mildly petulant)* Where have you been, La Ruse? You are later than usual. (CARTWRIGHT *sits* R. *of* L.C. *table.)*

LA RUSE. *(Coldly)* I doubted not but Mr. Cartwright was capable of amusing you.

LAETITIA. He has been reading me his verses; they are pretty verses. *(Roguishly, to* CARTWRIGHT*)* Are they not?

CARTWRIGHT. Pretty?

LA RUSE. If naught else damns you, Madam, your choice of adjectives will. I respect your gift, Mr. Cartwright. 'Twas a pity you were not here during the afternoon: the sunlight fell through the windows for a poet! Did I say poet? For more, sir: for lovers. (CARTWRIGHT *starts.)* Yes, 'twas a pity you weren't here.

CARTWRIGHT. *(Shortly)* I was writing in my room.

LA RUSE. *(Smiles)* Of love?

CARTWRIGHT. *(Sullen)* Perhaps.

LA RUSE. Youth, sir—youth is not thus to be served! *(He studies the boy's face)* Why, sir, because on such a day you should not have written of love—you should have enjoyed love!

CARTWRIGHT. You desire to affront me, La Ruse! *(Rises.* LAETITIA *sends him a frightened glance.)*

LA RUSE. Why should I desire to affront you, Mr. Cartwright? *(Down.)*

CARTWRIGHT. Because you do not like me, and because I do not like you.

LAETITIA. *(Very uneasy)* Gentlemen, gentlemen! Pray, what causes this sudden heat between you?

LA RUSE. We fight over truth and beauty, Madam. Perhaps more beauty than truth, since you are present.

LAETITIA. *(Angrily)* You are possessed, La Ruse! *(Rises; crosses* L. *to* CARTWRIGHT*)* Mr. Cartwright: pray, leave us—you'll find me here when you return!

CARTWRIGHT. *(Unwilling)* Would you have me withdraw—now?

LAETITIA. *(Firmly)* Now—now!—Until La Ruse is himself again! *(*LA RUSE *to down* R. CARTWRIGHT *goes out* L.*)*

LA RUSE. Harlot!

LAETITIA. Your language, La Ruse! I am not in a mood for these profane terms of endearment.

LA RUSE. Where were you this afternoon?

LAETITIA. Pray, if you've nothing better to say than this, say nothing.

LA RUSE. Where were you this afternoon? And where was Cartwright?

LAETITIA. Your silence will at the least be more genteel.

LA RUSE. *(To her)* You were both missing, all the afternoon! I cannot believe it possible, minx! Were you really with the boy?

LAETITIA. I was alone this afternoon, but what if I had not been alone, this or any other afternoon? Did you not tell me you should watch such a procedure with magnificent indifference?

LA RUSE. *(Characterised by the same sudden weariness which overcame him when with* MR. SNAP*)* I am not concerned for you. *(Crosses* R. *sofa.)*

LAETITIA. Your concern is not for me! La Ruse, you begin to lose your singular force when you are thus obvious: like a common lover, whose jaundiced eyes stain all things yellow, but mostly, those things which are not.

LA RUSE. *(Rather to himself)* The yellow merges into black; the shadow of a bird I saw. *(Sits sofa)* I am like an actor whose perfection in a role has forced him to play the part until it has become odious to him. My delight was the comedy of repetition; to say the same word, to make the same gesture, in separate delicate moments. And now—

LAETITIA. *(Spurs him)* And now, pray?

LA RUSE. I say the word, I make the gesture without the delight. I am resolved Mr. Cartwright shall be saved from a like fate. I discern in the poet's youth a talent more than mere youth. I would not have his quality debased by your merciless instincts. I would protect the shadow of my former self from your attractive ferocity.

LAETITIA. Your name, sir, your name? *(To sofa)* 'Tis highly improper for me to converse with a gallant whose name is unknown to me—although I perceive he is excellent, virtuous, angelic! One who protects widows, orphans, curates! Your name, your seraphic name, sir!

LA RUSE. Silence, trollop! *(Rises.)*

LAETITIA. La Ruse: you of a thousand crimes, thief, blackguard, ravisher! 'Tis a new penny-whistle you play me! 'Tis a new pamphlet by Mr. DeFoe cried on the streets: The Pope turns Protestant! The King preaches sedition! La Ruse turns evangelist!

LA RUSE. *(Controls himself)* Yes: the last lock I pick shall be on the gates of Paradise. I shall pick one or two before that, however. *(Crosses R.C.; sits.)*

LAETITIA. It seems that the creed of the church is lamentably insufficient. Pray, sir, will you not convert me to your peculiar creed? Your rival—in conversion—is Mr. Cartwright. He has promised to save me: my desolation shall bloom. We are to make love on the highways, which I learn is a far more marked virtuous way of making love than in private—

LA RUSE. *(Catches her up)* Ah! You have been making less virtuous love in private!

LAETITIA. 'Twas a mere figure of speech, such as you use often, and Mr. Cartwright.

LA RUSE. *(Viciously)* I would have wrung his juvenile neck for him, this afternoon. *(Takes her in his arms.)*

LAETITIA. *(Trills a few high notes)* I adore you, La Ruse. You were concerned with wringing his neck for him: not with saving his soul from me.

LA RUSE. I could not bear the thought of the cub in your arms. *(Despairingly)* I could not bear the thought! Yet why? What have I to do with what women do! Who are you—what are you, that your bawdiness causes my blood to choke my brain?

LAETITIA. *(Impatiently)* 'Tis the moment when your strict grammatical rule requires that you say you do not love me—though you do.

LA RUSE. Yes; in this chemical reality we must kiss evil on the mouth even as our spirits take flight from evil. *(Kisses her. Rises; crosses C.)* Like two wild horses, released by birth, body and soul strain different ways and tear us to pieces. 'Tis your pleasure— (LAETITIA *sits* R.C.) Madam, to whip the steeds o' myself until sense careens, but God be praised! your power is but the power of matter lacerating matter in a small confine, and I shall soon be out of that, I promise you. *(Looks at knife.)*

LAETITIA. I have a secret may keep you here longer than you think.

LA RUSE. Mr. Cartwright is no secret, and will not keep me here.

LAETITIA. Perhaps 'tis a new lock, of a special

sort, designed to keep you here! I will reveal my secret to you tomorrow—La Ruse.

LA RUSE. Tomorrow? I'll not be the sort of guest who's always leaving tomorrow. I shall make a more graceful exit—who knows—perhaps tonight.

LAETITIA. You talk as if you had some plan.

LA RUSE. Plan?—Never a day or a night goes by but I have some plan—

LAETITIA. You talk now—as if—

LA RUSE. As if?—Pray finish your sentence, madam!

LAETITIA. *(Rises)* I vow, La Ruse, because I was not to be found—because Mr. Cartwright was not to be found—

LA RUSE. *(Wryly)* Singular coincidence!

LAETITIA. You indulge in this wild talking of fleeing tonight! When you know 'tis but talk! Do you think the bolts will be weakened by your jealousy? For shame, sir! Would you be jealous of an impoverished poet?

LA RUSE. No: of an amorous day-dream.

LAETITIA. Believe whatever you will, I adore you. (LA RUSE *crosses* L.) La Ruse, you will confess that even though you are a Count—

LA RUSE. I am not a Count · I am a Marquis.

LAETITIA. *(The snob in her responding)* A Marquis! But, La Ruse! You are the strangest of men: you have withheld this from me all the while. Marquis! And one were your wife, *(Crosses; sits* R. *of table)* she would be a Marquise—only to think of that!

LA RUSE. You manage to seem a lady, until your veneration for a trumpery thus reveals you. I lowered my title, Madam, when I lowered my standards; an old family custom. My line, which began in a palace, ends in a jail.

LAETITIA. You are still a young man. 'Tis far from impossible—

LA RUSE. Shall I add another mouth to the pack? I have had one child—a bastard. Yes, I have withheld that also. He's a boy of ten by now, and thinks himself the son of an English lord, who is himself deceived, since he was deceived. I shall leave no issue with my name, and for this, much will be forgiven me on high.

LAETITIA. *(Earnestly)* 'Tis strange, La Ruse, you should talk thus at this jointure—'tis most strange! For 'twas in my thoughts to observe, when you interrupted, that although a Count—a Marquis, you are not much of a match today.

LA RUSE. What do you get at, Madam? 'Tis true, mothers with frumpish daughters no longer leer into my face. *(Sits on table.)*

LAETITIA. No: you are not much of a match today. Yet—if you were to ask me to marry you—

LA RUSE. Ask you to marry me!

LAETITIA. *(Quickly)* I should say yes, and force Papa's consent. (LA RUSE *rises.*) Ah! That was an unmannerly noise, La Ruse.

LA RUSE. *(Dazed)* Marry you! Marry you! Do you think because you have been my mistress you shall be my familiar? What! Are our bedfellows to answer us back? Monstrous presumption! What is your crest, Madam? Does it show bolts and bars against a field of human misery? Marry you! Marry you! Infamous affront to the blood royal in my veins!

LAETITIA. *(Serenely)* Truth to tell, you have taken the suggestion less violently than I thought you would. *(Rises; crosses R.)*

LA RUSE. There was a sovereign, Madam, once offered me the hand of his niece. I refused her, although the refusal must cause my downfall, as it did. I was fastidious: her ankles were confused with her leg. I am still fastidious, Madam; if in more elementary respects. Besides—

LAETITIA. *(Unflinching)* Besides, you think me untrue. *(Crosses L. to him)* I am not, La Ruse, and will prove it. Will you visit me tonight? Is't my fault if you force me to play the man in our courtship? I vow you regard me as something seen late at night in a cemetery!

LA RUSE. *(Horrified)* This afternoon—

LAETITIA. *(Exasperated)* This afternoon! I tell you 'twas no different from a thousand afternoons: dishes clattered and were still, the hot sun shone, a drowsiness filled the blue air, and I slept—as I always do.

LA RUSE. *(Vastly surprised)* As you always do? I thought you never slept, Madam! For I have noticed this peculiarity about you—your eyes are always open. You should see an oculist—one with a number of lenses: he will fit you with spectacles made for a wealthy tiger who failed to call back for them. The price is excessive, but the relief cosmological.

LAETITIA. *(Impatiently)* You are like the Prince in the play you will read me so often, though it bores me: words, words, words! Answer me, La Ruse, one way or t'other.

LA RUSE. Why should you desire me to visit you? I am like the Prince again: I have bad dreams.

LAETITIA. *(Softening)* I would dispel them.

LA RUSE. Yet 'tis whispered by mothers—you are the mother of nightmares.

LAETITIA. *(Clipping her words)* I grow weary of your reviling me.

LA RUSE. I have ever thought it strange myself that men should derive their refreshment from the weariness of women.

LAETITIA. *(In cold rage)* 'Tis too much! La Ruse, you shall learn I can repay far more than I am loaned!

LA RUSE. Rare creditor! I will have you done in oils and present the portrait to my banker.

LAETITIA. Hearken, La Ruse: you have imagined the poet in my arms; he shall be there. The lips you have tasted, he shall taste; the joy you have known, he shall know! I'll not have you sent back to the prison! I'll keep you here, where you shall see only that which you have cried, "I cannot bear!"—myself in the arms of another.

LA RUSE. (Struggles fiercely) It matters not! My spirit is strong to be free.

LAETITIA. (As the CLOCK strikes the hour) The torment of the night begins for you!

LA RUSE. (Ringingly) You are late, Madam, by the clock which strikes in Heaven! The hour of my deliverance is at hand.

LAETITIA. (Malefic) You are white already, La Ruse; you shall be grey with the grey dawn!

LA RUSE. (Exorcises her) Back to your inferno, devil!

LAETITIA. (Throws her fan on the table) 'Tis you return to the inferno—not I! Enough! You have set my course. (Exits C. rapidly.)

LA RUSE. (Breaking) Set her course!—'Fore God she'll do as she swears! Laetitia!

CARTWRIGHT. (Enters L. To C. opening) What new malice have you inflicted on her? And where is she gone?

LA RUSE. (Flicks a spot of dust from his coat) She has taken a fancy to Pluto, and is over the Styx by now.

CARTWRIGHT. Count La Ruse.

LA RUSE. Mr. Cartwright?

CARTWRIGHT. You are a scoundrel.

LA RUSE. Your opinion has had judicial recognition, sir. (To table.)

CARTWRIGHT. You have lied—

LA RUSE. Of Laetitia? To lie of Laetitia is as if

one were to speak the truth of another—the same affect is achieved.

CARTWRIGHT. *(Homicidal)* I'll blood you.

LA RUSE. *(Sits on table. Laughs)* You have sworn never to lay your hands on a human being, except in love. I would advise you not to lay your hands upon me, Mr. Cartwright. I am much the stronger of the two—and I may be armed.

CARTWRIGHT. *(Quietly, after a pause)* I never thought I should want to kill a man, but had I had my knife—

LA RUSE. Then I am obliged to the gentleman who took your knife.

CARTWRIGHT. And so am I, Count La Ruse.

LA RUSE. Besides, he has a use for it—tonight.

CARTWRIGHT. What would it profit me to throw myself at you? Mr. Wild is wicked; he can be killed. But you are evil, Count La Ruse, and evil must be killed by itself, or it does not die.

LA RUSE. The young rhetorician to the old rhetorician! *(Suddenly grave)* I know not why, Mr. Cartwright, but you make me speak not what I feel towards you, but the cutting opposite.

CARTWRIGHT. You are envious of me. sir.

LA RUSE. *(Sadly)* I am envious of you, not because of a woman, as you think, but because I am myself denied any special gift, and have, perhaps, too high a regard for the gifts of others. In my heart, Mr. Cartwright, I would be your friend.

CARTWRIGHT. Friend!

LA RUSE. Yes. 'Tis a sudden weakness of my past, an outbreak of paternity which ill-becomes my smile, I'll allow. I've a son, somewhere; I speak to you now as I would speak to him, were he your age.

CARTWRIGHT. You speak as a discredited rival.

LA RUSE. *(Loses his temper)* Rival? *You* my rival? With Laetitia? You! Is the pup in her lap my rival? You are still in your high-chair—pray, tighten your bib, the gruel spills on your flannel!

CARTWRIGHT. *(Laughs)* 'Tis as you said: you speak as a friend, as father to son.

LA RUSE. *(Checks himself)* I do, sir, but you goad me damnably. I'd not give much for the young man who succumbs to the ordinary hurt of first love, which is a sort of new teething we must all suffer. But you are in danger of a wound far more perverse, and therefore far more delicate! Heal yourself, before the fester penetrates beyond the heart and becomes permanent in the spirit.

CARTWRIGHT. Is not the very spice of affectation to appear more sincere than sincerity itself?

LA RUSE. Would you ham-string me on my own idle words? I implore you to heed me, lest you learn to your sorrow that there are women in whom the mother has been completely omitted, and that Laetitia is such a woman.

CARTWRIGHT. I have felt the mother in Laetitia comfort me.

LA RUSE. She could bear a kingdom, and never feel a maternal thrill! Take your light elsewhere, or 'twill go out like my own.

CARTWRIGHT. I have found that my light grows in her radiance, La Ruse.

LA RUSE. Mr. Cartwright: we are all of us defenseless when we love a good woman; how much more so when we love the implacable itself! But 'tis no use. A man, young or old, will as soon admit his secret body-odours as that the perfume of all creation is not in his new mistress! (CARTWRIGHT *starts.*) You started at the word: damme, but you did! Death-in-Hell! You confirm my suspicions! Is't really so?

CARTWRIGHT. I must know, before I reply, how you speak—as friend, as father to son, or—

LA RUSE. I stepped out of character for your

sake, but I speak as the Count La Ruse, lover of Laetitia!

CARTWRIGHT. And you speak to the poet Cartwright, lover of Laetitia!

LA RUSE. Whippersnapper!

CARTWRIGHT. Now I am a blackguard, but I feel better. *(Taunting him)* La Ruse: she loves me, she loves me, she loves me!

LA RUSE. Add she loves me not; that ends the rhyme always. You elephantine gods! where is your ancient nimbleness? Naught's divine, all's clownish, Mr. Cartwright: you do not believe I have been her lover?

CARTWRIGHT. Were I to believe that, I must believe—

LA RUSE. Laetitia has asked me to visit her tonight.

CARTWRIGHT. Your malice undoes you! She—

LA RUSE. Your silence undoes you: she's hinted you may visit her tonight. Well, I'll offer you this challenge for your soul: that Laetitia loves me, that we mirror each other, are bound to each other; that if I knock on her door tonight, she'll admit me! Do you take my challenge?

CARTWRIGHT. Do you think I would stoop to it?

LA RUSE. She'll admit me, I say, and where will you be? You'll be on the landing, outside her door: you'll be there with cold hands and a burning throat when your knock goes unanswered! Do you take my challenge?

CARTWRIGHT. No!

LA RUSE. I warned you once it would profit you more to cut the throat of Mr. Snap than to kiss the throat of his daughter. Well, poet and sweet-singer, tonight I shall do both! Yes, this shall be my final folly! I will risk my chance of freedom to prove a point of vanity.

CARTWRIGHT. Your point of vanity is my whole faith!

LA RUSE. Vanity or faith, there's a fire abroad which only your tears will put out! Do you take my challenge?

CARTWRIGHT. I take nothing, and I give nothing, but I hold fast to what I know.

LA RUSE. You do take my challenge. It must lie between us as men of honour.

CARTWRIGHT. As blackguards.

LA RUSE. Amen.

LAETITIA. *(Enters c.)* Ah, gentlemen, conversing most amiably, are you?

LA RUSE. Yes, we've been discussing the astronomical position of Venus tonight.

CARTWRIGHT. And of Lucifer.

LAETITIA. Leave him alone in his dark thoughts.

JONATHAN. *(Enters L.)* La Ruse! La Ruse!

LA RUSE. Well, Mr. Wild, what's on your mind?

JONATHAN. What's on my mind? Don't you know?

LA RUSE. Of course. You've decided?

JONATHAN. I'll take the risk. (MR. SNAP *enters* L.) Pay the full three hundred pounds. We'll stop in my room later—three hundred pounds. *(Crosses to chair L. of table L.C.)*   *(WARN Curtain.)*

MR. SNAP. What did he say? *(Crosses to* LA RUSE.)

LA RUSE. He'll pay the full one hundred pounds. (MR. SNAP *crosses to chair back of L.C. table.)* Whispering, Mr. Cartwright? *(Crosses to sofa)* I don't like whispering.

CARTWRIGHT. Then I'll whisper the whole night through.

LA RUSE. Better go to sleep in your narrow bed.

MR. SNAP. Well, gentlemen— *(Crossing a little to* R.) An amiable round of cards? (JONATHAN *sits*

chair L. *of card table.)* Will you join us— (JONA-
THAN *takes cards.)* Mr. Cartwright?

CARTWRIGHT. Thank you. I don't play.

MR. SNAP. *(Sits* R. *of card table)* Incredible, La
Ruse—he doesn't play.

LAETITIA. My fan—I'm sure I left in on the table
before— (CARTWRIGHT *crosses to above card table.)*

LA RUSE. I'll visit you tonight, wench. *(Crossing
to card table—sits* R.*)* Really, Mr. Cartwright, you
should have some amusement, and cards are your
only chance.

CARTWRIGHT. I might be tricked by the knave in
the pack.

MR. SNAP. Oh, come, sir, we are all honest. That
was a bad card you threw, La Ruse. I'll wager you
hold a bad hand.

LA RUSE. Yes, but I've a wager I hold a better
hand before the night is over.

CARTWRIGHT. The cards may not fall as you think,
La Ruse. (CARTWRIGHT *crosses up* C. LA RUSE *looks
at* LAETITIA, *who is singing lightly.)*

LA RUSE. *(Beams)* A mislaid fan, a daughter
singing, the men at the cards! They may say what
they want of felons and jailers, but where in all
Merrie England will you find a more domestic scene
than this? (LAETITIA *resumes her singing.)*

CURTAIN

ACT THREE

SCENE: *The same, next morning.*

MR. SNAP *enters* L. *with* LORD WAINWRIGHT, *a nobleman whose face is a chronic deadly white. His teeth are his most prominent feature; they protrude over his lip. His eyes are his least prominent feature; they are of that peculiar gray which seems to diffuse itself, the better to see. In his bearing, he has the genuine distinction of his class; and his speech is tinged with a hesitancy which is contradicted by the decisiveness of his thoughts.*

MR. SNAP. *(Cheerily)* Sit down, my lord, sit down! *(Dusting sofa)* You will stand? As you please. Is't not a fine morning, Lord Wainwright? I had my walk this morning. I wouldn't miss my walk on such a morning, my lord.

LORD WAINWRIGHT. I find myself totally uninterested in your pedestrian habits. *(Feels in his pockets)* Damn me, if some rascal in the jail hasn't relieved me of my snuff-box! Plague on him! The box was a masterpiece. I shall miss it.

MR. SNAP. 'Tis a pity, your lordship. You are well out of the jail, I'll warrant you. I marked you out of the mob at once— I saw at once you were a gentleman.

LORD WAINWRIGHT. *(Impatiently)* It is just as obvious that I am a gentleman as that you are not.

MR. SNAP. Your lordship!

LORD WAINWRIGHT. I must insist you abandon the cant of your kind, Mr. Snap. I have had enough of the cant of my own kind, since the day my mother told me a lying story of a stork and a chimney. *(Crosses down L.)* I am here because I finally took extreme measures to stop the flow of unmeaning talk around me. If you will not affect social compliments, but level your conversation to the mean quality of your nature, as 'tis apparent, you will find we will get along a great deal better. *(To fireplace)* I trust I have made myself plain.

MR. SNAP. Plain, my lord? Plain, did you say? I confess, I do not understand you.

LORD WAINWRIGHT. You found me in the jail; you offered me the privilege of being locked up in your home, instead.

MR. SNAP. Yes, I could not have offered you lodging yesterday; but fortunately Mr. Wild, *(Coughs)* vacates his room today.

LORD WAINWRIGHT. As your house could not possibly stink worse than the jail, I accepted your suggestion. Now, sir, what will you gouge me?

MR. SNAP. Gouge you, my lord! Did you say gouge you? You will find, Lord Wainwright, I am not avaricious.

LORD WAINWRIGHT. I see every evidence of avarice in your person. You brought me here to be well paid for your trouble.

MR. SNAP. *(Smarting)* And why not, my lord? Is't wrong I should be well paid for breaking the law? For chancing my official position? Is't wrong, my lord?

LORD WAINWRIGHT. 'Tis confoundedly right. Why do you not talk thus always? You would find me more amicable. I am well provided with money, Mr. Snap.

MR. SNAP. *(A little overcome by his honesty)* My lord!

LORD WAINWRIGHT. What privilege will my money buy for me?

MR. SNAP. For a reasonable sum you may buy the entire privacy of this floor.

LORD WAINWRIGHT. The sum will not be reasonable, and the floor will not be private, but I will buy it. The furnishings here are in the worst of taste; pray, is my bedroom of the same order?

MR. SNAP. 'Tis an exquisite room, your lordship. I furnished it myself, and I am—whatever rogues may say—a man of taste.

LORD WAINWRIGHT. I suspect our tastes differ. I am exceedingly fond of small objects, carved precisely—knick-knacks on which the eye may rest with pleasure. There is a want of them in this room, for instance.

MR. SNAP. My lord, we dare not leave them about. We have lodgers here not to be trusted. I should warn you against Mr. Wild, but he leaves *(Coughs)* this morning. Beware, however, of a scamp calling himself Count La Ruse. As for your knick-knacks, sir, chance has put one or two in my way; I hope to interest you in them.

LORD WAINWRIGHT. I'll have a look at them. I'll try to make myself as comfortable as possible until my trial.

MR. SNAP. Pray, my lord, may I inquire for what you are held?

LORD WAINWRIGHT. I thought I heard you inquire of the clerk in the prison?

MR. SNAP. I did, my lord, but I failed to catch his reply.

LORD WAINWRIGHT. *(Indifferently)* I poisoned my wife—and a few of her intimate friends.

MR. SNAP. *(Covers the shock with a silly laugh)* Dear me! Why did you do that?

LORD WAINWRIGHT. A gentleman does not discuss his family affairs with a vulgar stranger.

MR. SNAP. *(Not quite recovered)* Gentleman! 'Tis true—you seem such a gentleman.

LORD WAINWRIGHT. I am a lord, Mr. Snap, and would have you know that all the eminent poisoners were of good family; 'twas a symptom of their subtle breeding. You will do me the justice of not derogating my rank because I rid the world of a few useless people; a fact which, in any competent civilization, would indubitably raise my rank.

MR. SNAP. As for that, my lord, a lord is a lord to me, no matter what he's done. I hope I know the deference due to a man like yourself.

LA RUSE. *(Enters c. and stops short at sight of* LORD WAINWRIGHT) Lord Wainwright!

LORD WAINWRIGHT. I am equally astonished. Why, 'tis—

LA RUSE. *(Quickly)* Count La Ruse. I have long forgotten I had any other name, and must beg your lordship the favour of forgetting with me.

LORD WAINWRIGHT. Count La Ruse. *(Turns to* MR. SNAP ; *in a peculiar tone)* So this is your Count La Ruse! We are old acquaintances—are we not, Count?

MR. SNAP. A happy coincidence! You gentlemen will have the past to discuss. I'll go down below and see if there's a trace of some callers I'm expecting. *(Winks at* LA RUSE*)* Callers for Mr. Wild. *(He exits R.)*

LORD WAINWRIGHT. Pray, would you loan me your snuff, Count? My box was filched from me in the jail.

LA RUSE. And mine here. I'm starved for the powder. *(Crosses to c.)* Take heed you leave nothing of value where Mr. Snap can reach it. He's as unprincipled as a fox on the run.

LORD WAINWRIGHT. *(Permits himself a smile)* I

am obliged for the warning. Mr. Snap has been so good as to tender me a similar warning against yourself. I find myself amused.

LA RUSE. *(Unabashed)* I have been derelict in asking—how is your dear lady?

LORD WAINWRIGHT. *(Without emotion)* Dead.

LA RUSE. *(Shaken)* Dead!

LORD WAINWRIGHT. Quite dead. In fact, will never rise again. Did you think her ladyship would live forever? The expression of your face leads me to think you did.

LA RUSE. The news was unexpected. I remember her ladyship as an example of your fine English beauty, in which health is so much of the beauty. 'Tis hard to think of her dead. I tender you my deepest sympathy, Lord Wainwright.

LORD WAINWRIGHT. *(Passively)* Your sympathy is wasted: her ladyship's passing was a blessing, to me.

LA RUSE. I cannot believe you; there were not many like Lady Wainwright. With all respect, I was attached to her.

LORD WAINWRIGHT. You should be consoled by the knowledge, my dear Marquis, she was much attached to you.

LA RUSE. Yes, she did her best to save me from my many follies. May she rest in peace; she was a wise and charming lady.

LORD WAINWRIGHT. To her lovers. At home she was a bitch.

LA RUSE. *(Flares)* You make too free with your lady's memory!

LORD WAINWRIGHT. On my word, for a mere acquaintance, you are most concerned for my wife's good name! Is't possible you were more than a mere acquaintance of Lady Wainwright?

LA RUSE. I have not been unaware of your insinuations, sir; to answer them would be to dignify them. I have still some of the instincts of my breeding. *(Down to chair* R.C.*)*

LORD WAINWRIGHT. Cant! We have all the same instincts. Answer what you will, without cant.

LA RUSE. I will say this: you have a son, and when you degrade his mother, you degrade your heir. Sir, the passing of her ladyship may have been a blessing to you, but what a loss it must be to the boy! Do you not think of that? I glimpsed him in the park, not so many years ago; a golden-haired, rollicking boy.

LORD WAINWRIGHT. He will rollick no more.

LA RUSE. *(After a pause)* He is dead, also.

LORD WAINWRIGHT. Of the same distemper which removed his mother. (LA RUSE *sits chair* R.C.) By my honour, my dear Count—you have believed my family immortal. A boy dies, and there's such an expression on your face—

LA RUSE. And you—have you no regret for your son's passing?

LORD WAINWRIGHT. None at all. I never believed him to be my son.

LA RUSE. Not your son! But you brought him up.

LORD WAINWRIGHT. I played the father for a while, but the jest wearied me. It became intolerable a bastard should inherit my name and acres. The boy did not resemble me, not in the slightest.

LA RUSE. It scarcely becomes a man thus to slander his dead wife and her child.

LORD WAINWRIGHT. 'Tis exquisitely fitting I should meet you here and break the news; for a thought had often occurred to me; the boy was altogether of your type; had your head, eyes, mouth, gait and insufferable habit of talk, talk, talk.

LA RUSE. You knew— *(Rises; crosses to him)* all the while— You knew— Why are you held, Lord Wainwright?—You spoke of a distemper; what was this distemper?

LORD WAINWRIGHT. *(Brutally)* Arsenic.

LA RUSE. You— O! monster!

LORD WAINWRIGHT. And now the jest wearies you. I made little effort to conceal what I had done; to do so would have meant so much more of cant— hypocritical heavings of the breast, streaming tears, and lying eulogies. The funerals delighted me, and I let it be known. *(Crosses L.)*

LA RUSE. You are mad—stark mad, I perceive!

LORD WAINWRIGHT. So my lawyers say, but 'tis they who are mad, or they would not be lawyers. Pray, do me the favour of not intruding overmuch on my privacy here. I've a dislike for your company —always had, but at length can tell you so. *(During speech goes down round table to chair above table.)*

LA RUSE. *(Mechanically)* I leave this house forever this morning.

LORD WAINWRIGHT. One offense removed from my sight without my going to extremes. *(To fireplace.)*

MR. SNAP. *(Comes in from the hall R.)* What a day! What a day! Life's up and coming, gentlemen! You should see the gallants: they're winning the ladies everywhere, with insults; and the children, the happy children, are rollicking in the streets! What a day!

LA RUSE. *(Stabbed)* Rollicking!

MR. SNAP. I see you've been affected by your recollections with his lordship. There's nothing so pleasant as talking of old times. But you must accompany me now, La Ruse; the crowd gathers below already, and we must discuss, when Mr. Wild discovers— Pray, make yourself at your ease, my lord. (LAETITIA *has entered* C.)

LORD WAINWRIGHT. A wench! A pretty wench!

MR. SNAP. 'Tis my daughter, Laetitia. Daughter, this is Lord Wainwright, a new lodger in the house. His lordship's a real lord, and not one of your nobles born in a deck of cards and glass of whisky.

LAETITIA. *(Ingratiatingly)* 'Tis most pleasant to have you in the house, my lord. Good morning, La Ruse.

MR. SNAP. *(To* LA RUSE*)* Let us go. The moment arrives, and we've no plan— *(To door* R.*)*

LAETITIA. *(Piqued by* LA RUSE's *silence)* Do you set a new fashion, sir? Do you not say good morning? *(He makes a slight response)* I vow, if 'tis a good morning, you should admit the fact more graciously, I think.

MR. SNAP. By chance, Laetitia, Lord Wainwright's a great friend of Count La Ruse. (WAINWRIGHT *puts his hands over his ears and walks away.)*

LAETITIA. *(Gets a fuller view of* LA RUSE*)* Why, what ails you? You seem ill?

LA RUSE. *(Musters up a little of his usual manner)* Ill, Madam? Ill? I am well enough.

LAETITIA. Will you have a glass of spirits?

LA RUSE. *(Resenting her sympathy)* Thank you. There's no necessity.

MR. SNAP. *(Has been waiting; irritably)* But there's necessity for haste for both of us, sir! *(At door* R.*)* Are you rooted in the floor?

LAETITIA. Stay, Papa. I must know—what have you done further with Mr. Cartwright?

MR. SNAP. Further? Did you say further? The young rascal is locked in his room, and 'tis likely still feels the butt of my pistol on his face. In truth, I hope he does.

LAETITIA. 'Tis likely he meant less harm than we thought, Papa. I've forgiven him, this bright morning. I'm sure he's had nought to eat nor drink.

MR. SNAP. 'Twas you cried most "whip him! Scourge him! Lock him in his room! Send him back to the jail!"

LAETITIA. The early hour—the noise—the fighting—I was frightened. Since 'twas Love made him act thus, I owe him the duty of kindness.

La Ruse. *(Strangely)* He may kill you.

Laetitia. He's a boy, and easily handled.

Mr. Snap. *(Peremptorily)* La Ruse! *(Opens* r. *door)* You've wasted enough time. We must look to Mr. Wild, sir! *(*Wainwright *crosses down to chair* l. *of* l.c. *table.* La Ruse *goes out before him like a blind man who knows the way.* Mr. Snap *whispers to* Laetitia, *indicating* Wainwright*)* A poisoner! *(Exits* r.*)*

Laetitia. *(A spring released by the words)* Lord Wainwright! Pray, why is one of your station in such a place as this? *(Bows.)*

Lord Wainwright. Cant! Your father's whisper had all the discretion of a thunderclap. *(Sits* l. *of table)* Do you find me repulsive, now?

Laetitia. 'Twould be presumptuous indeed for me to find one of your station repulsive, my lord. *(Bows.)*

Lord Wainwright. We have our ugly faces.

Laetitia. No; far from finding you repulsive, *(Crosses to* r. *of table)* I'll confess that for me there's a titillating distinction in the thought you have poisoned people. I am no ordinary woman, my lord; I've lived so long in the atmosphere of a jail that I've come to measure my respect for men by the quality of their misdeeds; and yours would seem to belong in the very aristocracy of crime. Perhaps some day you will excite my ears with the history of your exploits. I should be ravished to hear them.

Lord Wainwright. *(Displeased)* For a wench you have a loathsome flow of words.

Laetitia. I have listened much to the conversation of your friend, Count La Ruse.

Lord Wainwright. I might have guessed.

Laetitia. Is he not your friend?

Lord Wainwright. Certainly not.

LAETITIA. But Papa said— *(Away a little* R.*)*

LORD WAINWRIGHT. Your father is a knave and a fool.

LAETITIA. You are plain-spoken.

LORD WAINWRIGHT. You will find me increasingly so, wench.

LAETITIA. For myself, I greatly admire Count La Ruse.

LORD WAINWRIGHT. I greatly despise him. A word-monger, I have had the courage to use a vial, and not a phrase.

LAETITIA. He has killed men and done worse with women— Papa has told me.

LORD WAINWRIGHT. He has had his moments— has aspired to be what I am; but there was a flaw in him he could not overcome; a belief in words—in cant! The world knows him as a villain. I know him as a sentimentalist.

LAETITIA. I thought all men were sentimentalists. *(Crosses to chair* R. *of table.)*

LORD WAINWRIGHT. All men but myself. I fight naked. *(Over table.)*

LAETITIA. You are a man with a mind of your own. *(Away* R.*)* And perhaps will find me a woman with a mind of her own.

LORD WAINWRIGHT. A plague on your mind! Do you think me interested in a woman's mind? I am not twenty, wench.

LAETITIA. Your lordship has called me so a number of times; my name is Laetitia, Mistress Laetitia.

LORD WAINWRIGHT. Your name is Laetitia, and you are still a wench.

LAETITIA. It pleases your lordship to affect an uncouthness which the refinement of your thought denies. *(Bows.)*

LORD WAINWRIGHT. Cant! Nothing but cant! I foresee I must undo the harm La Ruse has done you before I find your presence bearable.

LAETITIA. Your lordship flatters me with your courteous interest.

LORD WAINWRIGHT. My interest is always in myself. *(Casually)* I propose to enjoy your favours, wench.

LAETITIA. *(Left breathless)* My Lord! *(Away a little.)*

LORD WAINWRIGHT. Pray, spare me the cant of a lying outburst of your virtue. I can see in your eyes—

LAETITIA. *(His gaze forces hers to drop)* Did I ask you to look there, my lord—but not my master?

LORD WAINWRIGHT. It must be as patent to yourself as 'tis to me; you have been placed here for my convenience.

LAETITIA. And you think a woman like myself is to be won thus— *(Crosses to table; sits R. of it)* by being told she is to be a convenience?

LORD WAINWRIGHT. What do you wish of me? Repartee? Shall I speak like the world, of your eyes and the blue skies; your cheeks and the red rose— when all the while, like the world, I am thinking of a bed? I tell you, wench, I would live a celibate all of my days before a word of such cant should pass my lips to a woman.

LAETITIA. Your words have sealed your celibacy here involate, my lord—but not my master!

LORD WAINWRIGHT. I suppose you have some entanglement of a low order with one of the wardens of the prison, or stableboys there.

LAETITIA. Stableboy!

LORD WAINWRIGHT. No? Ah! You greatly admire Count La Ruse. 'Tis he, without a doubt. I'm lucky. He's told me he leaves the house this morning, not to return.

LAETITIA. A favorite notion of La Ruse's—without substance, my lord—but not my master.

LORD WAINWRIGHT. Then we will buy him off. He's threadbare, and will welcome the money.

LAETITIA. *(Her fingers drumming on the table)* Is this the sum of your courtship?

LORD WAINWRIGHT. No. For yourself— *(Over table)* I promise you shall have more money than you have ever had.

LAETITIA. *(Slaps his face)* Filthy beast!

LORD WAINWRIGHT. *(Wipes his face thoroughly)* I thought you a woman of sense.

LAETITIA. Of too much sense—to sell what can never be bought back.

LORD WAINWRIGHT. Cant! You have nothing to sell of the nature. Where is your room? *(Rises)* I'll visit you this very night.

LAETITIA. *(Rising. Passionately)* On the first floor of the moon! Seek it there. You'll not come closer, Lord Wainwright!

LORD WAINWRIGHT. Where is your room, wench? You'll not say? Then I must bribe your father to give me ingress.

LAETITIA. I promise, nay I swear; if ever you so much as gain ingress over my threshold—I'll recant all I have said, I'll own you for my lord and master.

LORD WAINWRIGHT. A dangerous promise, wench.

LAETITIA. A safe promise. What your crimes could not do, your manners have done. I find you repulsive. I hate you! I hate you!

LORD WAINWRIGHT. *(Smiles)* Then I have accomplished the beginning of my end. Pray, don't run because of me. I'm content for the moment and will seek my own room. Perhaps you'll tell me where it lies, wench? *(To door L.)*

LAETITIA. I am not your servant.

LORD WAINWRIGHT. You shall be more. *(Flings door open L.)* Adieu, from your lord—and master. *(He exits L.)*

LAETITIA. *(Her fists clenched)* Turk! Mohammedan! *(Crosses up; sits sofa.* CARTWRIGHT *comes in* L. *There is a large bruise on his forehead, and in his eyes the look of a man who has seen things clear, too suddenly, and is a little strange as a result. He stops short at sight of* LAETITIA, *then bows with exaggerated deference.)*

CARTWRIGHT. *(With a peculiar purring softness)* Good morning, Mistress Laetitia. *(To chair* R. *of table.)*

LAETITIA. You! And now you must plague me! It has not been enough—

CARTWRIGHT. It makes me most happy to see you, *(Crosses to her a little)* dear lady, charming as always. I trust you slept well?

LAETITIA. Impudence! If I did not sleep well 'twas because of your infant outburst.

CARTWRIGHT. *(Smoothly)* I greatly regret having incommoded you, Mistress Laetitia. (LAETITIA *rises. Crosses to chair* R.C.) Is it not a delicious day? *(Down a little)* May I hope, presently, to have your hand in the dance? I've been told your minuet is as irreproachable as my own.

LAETITIA. Pray, what is this nonsense you babble? I am not in a mood for it, I warn you.

CARTWRIGHT. 'Tis not nonsense, but an event of world-shaking importance. I have become a very discreet gentleman; my manners now are exquisite.

LAETITIA. Cant! *(Amazed at her use of the word, and tut further out of temper by it)* And now you have the audacity to make game of me. I'll speak with you, Mr. Cartwright, when you've apologized for your behaviour. *(Crosses to* C. CARTWRIGHT *stops her.)*

CARTWRIGHT. I do not make game of you, Madam. We play a game together. Pray, would you leave me when the game's just begun?

LAETITIA. *(Back a little)* You're inexcusably young. I'll humour you. *(Sits sofa.)*

CARTWRIGHT. *(To sofa)* The game's called cat-and-mouse; and as you played cat before, you must play mouse now—as is only fair, you'll be the first to admit.

LAETITIA. You played cat enough last night—clawing La Ruse as you did! You—you who swore —"I will do, always, whatever you ask me!"

CARTWRIGHT. And so I will, dear lady. *(Crosses to Left.)*

LAETITIA. Pray, were you demented? What was your reason—nay, where was your reason? Falling on La Ruse at three o'clock in the morning—

CARTWRIGHT. *(Punctilious)* At three-seventeen.

LAETITIA. Falling on him in the hall—

CARTWRIGHT. *(More intensely)* As he left your room—

LAETITIA. Causing a hullabaloo—bringing Papa out with a whip and pistol— *(Rises; crosses L.)* When you knocked, I persuaded you to return to your room. Why did you leave it again?

CARTWRIGHT. I did not leave my room. My room left me. (LAETITIA *over L. a little.)* Pray, Madam, have you ever had the floor drop from under you? The sensation is unique.

LAETITIA. Your talk was always bizarre, but I vow 'tis now altogether lacking in sense, Mr. Cartwright.

CARTWRIGHT. 'Tis sense that your father believes I would have ravished you but for the heroic interference of Count La Ruse. Yes, 'tis sense, but is't not also most bizarre? *(Sits sofa.)*

LAETITIA. Do you think I'm unaware how hard it must be to forgive me for that lie? *(Crosses to sofa and sits)* But what else could I do?

CARTWRIGHT. *(With sudden plaintiveness)* But you cried, "Whip him! Scourge him!" Why did you want me beaten harder than I was beaten?

LAETITIA. I was fearful lest you should cry out—

what you knew. Shame and grief consume me—
Why should you listen to me now—though I speak
the truth at last?

CARTWRIGHT. *(Impulsively)* Tell me only this:
when we were alone together, and I felt your softness—was it true then?

LAETITIA. I'll not deceive you; 'twas partly true.
Pray, do not despise me too much. Why should you
believe that La Ruse forced his way into my room—
That he was never my lover before, and will never
be again? Even now, when I speak the truth at last,
you are right to put no faith in me.

CARTWRIGHT. I should not have looked into your
eyes—

LAETITIA. Have you forgotten so soon— (CART-
WRIGHT *rises.)* drawn shades, and open lips? Were
you to lie in my arms now, my softness should all be
true, and lasting, and still.

CARTWRIGHT. Hearts loud, and life still. *(Bends
over her proffered mouth, and bursts into laughter)*
Cat-and-mouse! Who's cat now? Who's mouse?
(Away to down R.)

LAETITIA. *(Stupefied)* You'll not kiss me?

CARTWRIGHT. Kiss you! In broad daylight? We
might be seen, Madam.

LAETITIA. This is witchcraft— *(Rises)* You speak
no longer like yourself, but like La Ruse.

CARTWRIGHT. *(Cunningly)* Because I'm no longer
a cat. 'Tis said, there are no more wolves in England, but most ignorantly, Madam; there are no
more men; we are all wolves.

LAETITIA. Your eyes burn me, I vow, like a wild
animal's! Pray, recollect—I'm a female—your gen-
tility—

CARTWRIGHT. Do you but let down your hair, dear
lady, and you'll see me eat it, ravenously.

LAETITIA. *(Forced to settee)* I'll call for help—
(Crosses to door R.)

CARTWRIGHT. *(Laughs. Crosses to her* R. *Pushes her toward sofa)* You will only call in more wolves. *(Prosaically)* 'Tis strange, dear lady, how lovely you are. I've seen all beasts, clear or striped, but you are the most beautiful beast I have ever seen.

LAETITIA. *(Has the courage of one at bay)* You'll be whipped for these insults! *(Pushes her.)*

CARTWRIGHT. *(With melancholy wonder)* Why should your eyes seem different from other eyes? You are loved madly, Madam.

LAETITIA. Aye, madly! Think of what you do, Mr. Cartwright—you'll regret later—

CARTWRIGHT. You have brought love to my heart, tears to my eyes, and a great rage to my brain. Where's peace, now? What death must I live—and you die?

LAETITIA. No more—let me pass at once—at once— (LAETITIA *tries to escape.)*

CARTWRIGHT. *(Pushes her on sofa)* I will do, always, whatever you ask me. *(Strokes her hair)* Shall I twist this around your throat, tightly—in the charming Italian fashion? I will do, always, whatever you ask me. Will you ask me to whip you, scourge you? Pray, ask me to kill you, Madam. I will do, always, whatever you ask me. *(The terrified* LAETITIA *sees* LA RUSE *enter* R.*)*

LAETITIA. *(Imploringly)* La Ruse! La Ruse! (CARTWRIGHT *crosses; sits chair* L. *of table* L.C.)

LA RUSE. *(Hastens)* What's this?

CARTWRIGHT. *(Turns)* La Ruse?

LAETITIA. *(Runs by him)* He would have killed me!

CARTWRIGHT. *(Laughs)* Saved again, by your nocturnal hero!

LAETITIA. He would have killed me!

LA RUSE. Alas! I am punctual only when 'twould have been better never to have arrived.

LAETITIA. I'll have him flayed alive.

LA RUSE. Do you not see, the boy's in travail?
(Takes her hand) Hearken to me, Madam. You'll
not say a word; the boy has suffered enough.

LAETITIA. *(In utter caprice, smiles at the poet)*
Of course I'll not say a word! Do you know, Mr.
Cartwright, I begin to like you. I begin to like you
very much, since feeling your violent hand.

LA RUSE. You hear this woman, Mr. Cartwright?
Why did you let me distract you? (MR. SNAP *enters*
R.)

LAETITIA. *(Quickly)* No more, now.

MR. SNAP. *(Jubilant)* 'Tis done, La Ruse! 'Tis
well done! 'Tis all prepared, sir!

LAETITIA. What's all prepared, Papa? The money
you've promised me for my new bonnet? *(Down* C.
a little.)

MR. SNAP. She'll have her money; won't she, La
Ruse?

LA RUSE. The bailiffs have come for Mr. Wild.
He hangs directly. *(Sits sofa.)*

MR. SNAP. *(A little over to sofa)* He's left you a
legacy, daughter: your new bonnet, and a kerchief
or two for myself as well. The payment's over and
done with already. *(To* LA RUSE—*then crosses
down* R.*)* They'll seize him as he comes down the
hall. (WILD *comes in* L. *The appalled* SNAP *darts
behind* LA RUSE'S *back.)*

JONATHAN. *(Is in a state of perspiring agitation)*
Mr. Snap! Mr. Snap! Where's Mr. Snap? *(Crosses
R.)*

MR. SNAP. *(Emerges haltingly)* Your servant,
Mr. Wild. What can I do for you? Pray, command
me.

JONATHAN. I've been talking with Lord Wainwright—says you said I'm to vacate my room at
once— I'm pardoned, am I not? The money's passed
and I'm pardoned?

MR. SNAP. *(Obeys* LA RUSE's *nod)* Aye, you're pardoned, Mr. Wild.

JONATHAN. *(Gasps)* Why didn't you tell me?

MR. SNAP. The pardon's but here— I was on the point of rushing to your room—

JONATHAN. Is't a complete pardon?

MR. SNAP. Aye, a complete pardon.

JONATHAN. O, God! They're not going to hang me—they're not going to hang me. They're not going to hang me!

MR. SNAP. Let us adjourn to my office. (CART-WRIGHT *rises; goes up stage.)* Some few minor details of the pardon still must be settled between us.

JONATHAN. Details, sir? Details in your mouth mean money. If 'tis more money you want, you'll not have it— I've paid all that I will pay, and more. *(Crosses to* MR. SNAP.)

MR. SNAP. 'Tis not money, sir. But in a case like your own, there's this and that must be settled before all's concluded according to the law's niceties—

LORD WAINWRIGHT. *(Enters* L., *carrying fan. Speaks as* MR. SNAP *speaks)* This is not a prison but a bazaar of the arts. I've a gift for you, wench. *(Crosses to her; shows the fan.* WILD *and* MR. SNAP *depart* R.)

LAETITIA. *(Snatches the fan)* My fan! I missed it last night!

LORD WAINWRIGHT. Mr. Wild sold me the fan for his wife's. I find myself amused! *(Crosses* L. *A horrible CRY is heard in the hall* R.—*the cry of a beast who has stumbled into a trap.* MR. SNAP *runs in.)*

MR. SNAP. Lord, he's a bulky fellow, and tussles arrantly! *(The sound of the FIGHT passes from the hall to the adjoining room.)* They don't dare use their pistols on him; he'd rather be shot than hanged.

JONATHAN. *(Straining against the two* BAILIFFS

who hold him, is seen at the R. *door, where they get him in hand. Wildly)* Gulled! Gulled! Villains! Assassins! Curse you! Curse you! My money! My money! My life! My life!

MR. SNAP. *(Merrily)* Taste! Did you say I'd no taste, sir? You'll get your walk in the air today, sir!

JONATHAN. *(Half fainting, as he is led away)* O, God! They're going to hang me—someone stop them —someone help me— O, God! Someone help me. (LAETITIA *exits* C.)

MR. SNAP. Aye, help him for the rogue of rogues! I must attend him to the gallows; 'tis not the hardest duty I've done. *(Exits* R.*)*

CARTWRIGHT. Wild is an odious man, but I pity him.

LORD WAINWRIGHT. Pray, who is this warm-hearted young man? Must I endure his charitable impulses, with all the rest?

LA RUSE. Mr. Cartwright, a poet. Lord Wainwright, a poisoner.

LORD WAINWRIGHT. I detest poets.

CARTWRIGHT. And I detest poisoners. *(Crosses to window and watches. The CATCALLS of a crowd below rise thickly.)*

LORD WAINWRIGHT. Interminable cant! Well, I've one comfort; I've a snuff-box again. *(Takes a pinch.)*

LA RUSE. *(Tries to see the box)* A snuff-box again! Pray, my lord, I'm dying for a pinch. *(Crosses to* WAINWRIGHT L. WAINWRIGHT *hands him the box.)* My snuff-box!

LORD WAINWRIGHT. Yours! Am I swindled again?

LA RUSE. Yes. Who sold you the article? Mr. Snap?

LORD WAINWRIGHT. Mr. Wild! You must prove this, sir, for you're as great a thief as the others.

LA RUSE. *(Traces the lines)* My monogram. You must look close—'tis hidden in the design.

LORD WAINWRIGHT. Cunningly: I never noticed. This fails to amuse me.

CARTWRIGHT. *(As another shower of CAT-CALLS rises)* He's in the cart now, and the cart starts—

LA RUSE. God speed! *(Crosses* L.*)*

CARTWRIGHT. The mob follows—

LA RUSE. 'Tis a pity they do not follow Wild as far as he goes! I'll paraphrase one of your potentates, sir: "O! That the world had but one neck, that I might hang it!"

LORD WAINWRIGHT. *(Glares at* LA RUSE*)* One must envy Mr. Wild: he'll soon be stone-deaf! *(Exits* L.*)*

CARTWRIGHT. Count La Ruse. *(Down to* C.*)*

LA RUSE. Mr. Cartwright?

CARTWRIGHT. I owe you an apology, sir.

LA RUSE. *(Surprised)* For what, pray?

CARTWRIGHT. For attacking you.

LA RUSE. You were belaboured enough for that.

CARTWRIGHT. And for my behaviour in general.

LA RUSE. We must all apologize for that.

CARTWRIGHT. You are generous.

LA RUSE. I am sad—sad at the thought that you must remain here while I have at last found a way to freedom: I leave this morning. Have you no possible means of imitating me soon?

CARTWRIGHT. *(Looks into the sky)* Can I fly on the wings of those white birds?

LA RUSE. White birds! Do they fly again? Then you are safe. I have discovered they are the true omens of hope.

CARTWRIGHT. *(Cries out)* Their talons tear me.

LA RUSE. You are torn by your own talons. My friend, my son—more than you guess, my son now—you must not give way. No matter how often we are born, it is always in pain. You have become a man, and must prepare to act as a man.

CARTWRIGHT. *(Passionately)* Act as a man! I know what you mean, and my heart tells me 'tis a lie. Because I must lean a little awry, be a little dirty, I am a man! Do you think because a woman has smiled or not smiled I'll throw acid on the world? Have I been burned terribly? I'll thrust my hand deeper into the flame.

LA RUSE. I rejoice, for I perceive in you a strength which I lacked.

CARTWRIGHT. *(With sudden gloom)* My strength will die, for here the flame is infernal. To be held here—

LA RUSE. Ah, here! Yes— *(Sits on table.)*

CARTWRIGHT. There's a witch in this house; she's sworn to teach me the joy of yellow-tinged things. *(Crosses down R.)*

LA RUSE. You must not permit—

CARTWRIGHT. The inevitable! Do you think, because I am a poet, I am less than a man?

LA RUSE. I think, because you are a poet, you should be more than a man.

CARTWRIGHT. Time and loneliness will make me less—here. I'll shut myself in my room. I'll work. And always I'll hear light feet passing in the hall.

LA RUSE. *(Excitedly)* I forbid you to hear them.

CARTWRIGHT. I'll hear them, always. One day, or one night, I'll fling my pen aside—I'll run, I'll throw myself into her open arms—

LA RUSE. *(Anguished)* They'll not release you until you've taken her very mold! You are right: the rest is too awful. 'Tis rankly unfair. Could I but do something for you—

CARTWRIGHT. I am lost for two hundred pounds.

LA RUSE. *(Starts)* Two hundred pounds! I'll— *(Lays his hand on his pocket and removes it angrily. Down a little)* Why the devil do you tell me your woes? Because a life is ruined, a talent despoiled, shall I be troubled? Take your own medicine, sir; what's your sickness to do with me? I am well again! Pray, take yourself where I won't pity you for the brief moments I remain: I despise myself for my pity. *(Crosses to L.)*

CARTWRIGHT. *(Mildly)* I'll trouble you no further. You have tried to be my friend in a friendless place. Will I see you again?

LA RUSE. I'll make it a point. But stay— Yes, I can do something for you. I've a little token of hope you shall have of me now. *(Hands CARTWRIGHT his knife.)*

CARTWRIGHT. The knife!

LA RUSE. 'Tis the most I can do for you.

CARTWRIGHT. You have given me a brave testimonial of friendship, and I shall thank you—by using it bravely.

LA RUSE. But not rashly. If the moment comes—when you fling your pen aside—I would have you strike clean. 'Twould be the last honour you could pay to life.

CARTWRIGHT. I will aim for my heart.

LA RUSE. The thought pierces my own, but you will do well. *(The CLOCK strikes the hour. CARTWRIGHT puts knife in pocket.)* And now, I must look to my luggage.

CARTWRIGHT. I'll await your call in my room. *(Goes out L. LA RUSE, with an effort, puts him from mind; is attracted to the window.)*

LA RUSE. *(Tenderly)* White birds! I shall fly with you after all.

LAETITIA. *(Enters C.)* La Ruse. *(Crosses L.)*

LA RUSE. Madam? *(Crosses L.)*

LAETITIA. You've been most ungallant this morning. You'd scarcely greet me, when you should have thanked me.

LA RUSE. *(Raising his eyebrows)* Thanked you?

LAETITIA. For last night. Of late you have grown obtuse, my lover.

LA RUSE. Of late I have grown wise, Madam.

LAETITIA. If weariness is wisdom.

LA RUSE. It may well be.

LAETITIA. *(To above table)* I promised you should hear my secret this morning, La Ruse.

LA RUSE. *(Enjoying himself to the full)* You may keep it forever now. Your business is no longer my business. You'll not scoff when you hear my secret: I've money to pay my debt. You still scoff? Madam, can you count beyond your fingers? *(Shows her the money.)*

LAETITIA. *(Thunderstruck)* How did you get this money?

LA RUSE. 'Twas like your new bonnet: an unwitting legacy from the lamented Great Jonathan. Two hundred pounds for my debt, and fifty for a nest-egg. When your father hears this he'll double up with a belly-ache, but he can do naught. I have the honour, Mistress Snap, to bid you an eternal farewell.

LAETITIA. *(Bites her lips)* You can't leave, La Ruse! You must first hear what I say.

LA RUSE. I have given thought to your remarkable words of yesterday, and have guessed your secret, Madam. *(They look at each other. She sees that he has.)*

LAETITIA. *(Sits R. of table)* Have you no feeling? Would you desert me—

LA RUSE. Your secret will speed me on my way.

LAETITIA. *(Flares)* Not when Papa knows—

LA RUSE. I am down on the books for debt, Madam. When that debt is paid, I'll laugh at your papa for the father of a strumpet. I am free of you until the North Star turns South for warmth.

LAETITIA. Cant!

LA RUSE. *(Struck by this)* Cant! Did you say

cant? The monster Wainwright has made an impression. I foresee my successor.

LAETITIA. *(Shivers)* No, never that horrible man! He terrifies me, La Ruse. I have never met such a man.

LA RUSE. Have you at last met a man who terrifies you? I may yet be revenged.

LAETITIA. Do not say that! The cold passion of that man has made me feel, for the first time in my life, as if I need a protector. I beseech you, La Ruse, do not depart now.

LA RUSE. I am not in a mood—to stay. Goodbye, Laetitia.

LAETITIA. *(Rises)* Go, then! Do you think I'll not be consoled for your loss? There are means at hand—

LA RUSE. Lord Wainwright?

LAETITIA. Do not name him! But the poet—

LA RUSE. He terrified you, also.

LAETITIA. Only for an instant. Do you forget, you once made the same gesture? 'Tis over with him as quickly as 'twas with you. Cartwright is but a doll with your features, and I'm not a woman of my mind if I can't dress him in your clothes—lend him your peculiar charm—paint your smile on his face! Already, he begins babbling like yourself.

LA RUSE. *(Loses his composure)* Infernal woman!

LAETITIA. Within a week, or a fortnight, I'll think I talk to you when I talk to him. Oh, I can draw your pattern, La Ruse—cut the pretty doll to your elegant vile shape; for 'tis the shape, alas, I adore.

LA RUSE. Infernal woman! If I thought you'd succeed—

LAETITIA. You'll be far away. *(Crosses down L.)* I vow, La Ruse, you haven't told me where you go.

LA RUSE. I go nowhere. When I leave this house

—Count La Ruse is no more. I take ship at once for the colonies. There—

LAETITIA. There—you will be what you are here.

LA RUSE. *(Violently)* No.

LAETITIA. *(Pityingly)* Do you think you can kill La Ruse in yourself? *(Sits)* 'Tis late, my lover, for a new marriage of the elements.

LA RUSE. You lie.

LAETITIA. 'Tis to be seen. Take ship for the colonies! What will you do? Work in the Carolina rice-fields with the slaves? But you'll never reach the dock. No. I'll describe your route for you from the prison door. You'll pause at a tavern for a bumper of liberty; 'twill lead to another bumper. A wench will catch your eye; you'll toy with her and have half a mind to do more; you'll have another bumper, and you'll do more. This will lead to a bumper of repentance; and as by this time your funds are depleted, you must try your luck at the tables. There you'll be stripped, and as your ship sails you'll be meditating some purse-cutting expedition. From this meditation 'tis but a short step to your return here. Yes, you're old to play a new part; you'll find it easier to don a costume which fits, and speak lines you know.

LA RUSE. Devil, I could almost believe you! What if I should be returned here? What if I should find an echo of myself—where I had left a poet?

LAETITIA. You will, La Ruse, I promise you.

LA RUSE. Infernal woman! You've put thoughts into my head—

LAETITIA. 'Tis palpable someone must.

LA RUSE. Damn you for a lying harlot! *(Crossing to above table)* I'm off when your father returns.

LAETITIA. You can't leave before, and perhaps not then. I'll downstairs and tell him—what I have to tell him. I'll wager, debt or no debt, he keeps you here. *(Crosses R.)*

LA RUSE. *(Savagely)* Let him try!

LAETITIA. You're a fool, sir, but I love you—more than the poet who'll sing my praises if you do leave; the poet whom I'll cut to your pattern! *(She laughs; exits R.)*

LA RUSE. *(Stares after her)* Cut to my pattern! She'll do't, by God, she'll do't! *(He comes to a dozen decisions in as many moments: he suffers his passion)* Too old to play a new part! *(His passion grows, and reaches a climax; he accepts his fate, goes to door L. and calls)* Mr. Cartwright! Mr. Cartwright! *(CARTWRIGHT comes in. LA RUSE faces him with an air of amazed joy.)*

CARTWRIGHT. You are leaving?

LA RUSE. You are leaving, sir!

CARTWRIGHT. *(Incredulous)* I am leaving?

LA RUSE. We are both leaving. I've had the most extraordinary communication, within the minute.

CARTWRIGHT. But tell me—

LA RUSE. *(Pirouettes)* Shout! Laugh! Sing! The world is ours again.

CARTWRIGHT. But tell me—

LA RUSE. True, I must tell you. I've mentioned my son: we've been parted by my escapades. I've just heard from his guardians: they've come to my rescue. Yes, I'm about to be everlastingly reconciled to my son: he's come into a vast and beautiful estate, is rich without measure! And I'm to share in his new wealth. You're held for a beggarly two hundred pounds: here's the sum, and fifty pounds additional for your needs. Now, sir, will you believe at last in white birds?

CARTWRIGHT. *(Dazed)* 'Tis perhaps the difference to me between life and death, fame and infamy— I'll not be coy over taking the money—

LA RUSE. I was not coy over taking the money myself!

CARTWRIGHT. I rejoice at your own good fortune, Count La Ruse.

LA RUSE. I rejoice at it myself. I would have you have a token of mine for remembrance. Will you accept this snuff-box?

CARTWRIGHT. *(Overwhelmed)* I've nothing to give in return.

LA RUSE. No? I would like a token. The knife! You'll not need it now, and 'twas yours when first we met; 'twill be a lively memento of our time together. Will you let me have it back? *(Turns back on* C.*)*

CARTWRIGHT. *(Gives him knife)* Of course. 'Tis likely I can never repay you; but were I able, where should I reach you?

LA RUSE. Write me—damn me if I know my new address! I've forgotten—'tis a strange one. Write me care of Mr. Snap: I delay to fee him to forward my letters. Run, sir! Joy awaits you.

CARTWRIGHT. And you?

LA RUSE. I am a little too old for joy, but peace will perhaps serve me better.

CARTWRIGHT. You have truly been a father to me, Count La Ruse.   *(WARN Curtain.)*

LA RUSE. Would you greatly mind if I give you a father's parting benediction? *(He kisses him.)*

CARTWRIGHT. There are tears in your eyes.

LA RUSE. The tears of reconciliation with my son—and with parting from you. *(Goes* R.*)* I've grown overly fond of you, sir. And now, like a true father who's never been wise in his own life, I'll instruct you how to be wise. Take no man's advice, love no woman too much. When you come to the shade, as you will, do not disparage it because you have seen the sun: there may be wonders in the darkness. Farewell.

CARTWRIGHT. *(Rises; crosses* R.; *shakes hands)*

Farewell!—If I could say something more—to show my gratitude! I shall write a sonnet to you, if I may. *(Exits R.)*

LA RUSE. Sonnet to me! 'Twill be my fate, 'tis one of his minor works. *(But with this his mask perishes; he walks to the window and stands as he stood a short while before)* It must be a black bird, after all—

LAETITIA. *(Enters R. Wide-eyed)* O, fool! fool! Given him your money—freed him in your place— O, fool! O, fool! sentimental fool!

LA RUSE. *(Walks to the R. door heavily)* 'Tis the only wise thing I have ever done. There have been too many hairs on my shoulder—

LAETITIA. *(With an evil smile)* Now you belong to me—forever.

LA RUSE. Now I am free forever. *(He goes out R. LAETITIA wonders. The THUD of a body falling is heard in the hall. She runs, sees, retreats into the room, incapable of an outcry.)*

MR. SNAP. *(Enters C. Chuckling)* 'Twas an expeditious hanging. What is it, Daughter? *(She points R.; he exits into the hall and returns, awed)* Stabbed himself—clean through the heart.

LAETITIA. *(Finds voice; beats hysterically on her father's breast)* I'll strangle his child— I'll strangle his child in my womb—

MR. SNAP. *(Seizes her hands; looks up at her, a great fear in his face)* His child! (WAINWRIGHT appears L. LAETITIA collapses in her father's arms.)

WAINWRIGHT. *(Assists him in picking up her limp form)* Pray, Mr. Snap, show me into her room— I must have ingress into her room.

THE END

CHILDREN OF DARKNESS

PROPERTY PLOT

ACT I

Ledgers.
Papers.
Ink-pot.
Quill pens.
Money.
Manacles.
Document.
Snuff-box.
Silver locket.
Knife.

ACT II

Spinet.
Fan.
Knife.
Playing cards.
Candles.

ACT THREE

Fan.
Knife.
Money.

CHILDREN OF DARKNESS

PUBLICITY THROUGH YOUR LOCAL PAPERS

The press can be an immense help in giving publicity to your productions. In the belief that the best reviews from the New York and other large papers are always interesting to local audiences, and in order to assist you, we are printing below several excerpts from those reviews.

To these we have also added a number of suggested press notes which may be used either as they stand or changed to suit your own ideas and submitted to the local press.

"Probably the best comedy ever written by an American."—*The Nation.*

"A style that is as unique in the theatre as out of it—belongs to the authentic tradition of high comedy."—*New York Evening Post.*

"I enjoyed 'Children of Darkness' immensely. There are gorgeous lines, gorgeous gestures, gorgeous verbal indiscretions. There is bitterness and there is beauty; there is wisdom and there is mockery."—*New York Telegram.*

"Mr. Mayer writes with distinction. There are flashes of poetry, a very unusual felicity of rhetoric. Altogether a novel entertainment, and decidedly superior—to what usually appears on Broadway— Here was all the beauty, seductiveness, impudence." —*New York Herald-Tribune.*

"It is a sly play for such rowdy characters, but deft, witty and immensely flavorsome, full of shrewd humor and slick writing— A zestful evening of uncommon quality."—*New York Journal*.

"It is a smouldering story, grim with underworld humor."—*New York American*.

"A handsome, amusing and rather extraordinarily contrived comedy— An enamel is this 'Children of Darkness,' a glowing, colorful and well wrought enamel. I am grateful for its production."—New *York Telegraph*.

"The play, written in the freest and best poetic prose of which the gratefully remembered author of 'The Firebrand' is capable— Rarely philosophical and richly satirical—"—*New York Daily News*.

"Edwin Justus Mayer, in his second play, has achieved something extraordinary in the vein of artificial comedy— What was irony and contemporary satire in Fielding becomes, at Mr. Mayer's hands, an independent study in malice, 18th Century in manner but modern in point of view, and as far from Congreve, Goldsmith or Sheridan as Andreyev and Strindberg and the prophets of disillusion. It is no idle pastiche; it is a play on the terms Mr. Mayer selected— From 'The Firebrand' of 1924 to 'Children of Darknes' of 1930 is the measure of Mr. Mayer's maturity as an artist— The style of the writing and the craftiness of the humors represent distinguished talent."—*New York Times*.

"In 'Children of Darkness,' Mr. Edwin Justus Mayer has written a literary play that acts— 'Children of Darkness' not only has a cultivated eloquence particularly distinctive in a day given to the cliches of naturalism in the theatre, but is a play that combines the heartiness, the cynical elegance and the cold, jesting cruelty of the early 18th Century English dramatists with something of the modern spirit, in the way which keeps it from seeming a mere imitation of the early Hanoverian playwrights. Mr. Mayer's drama is a distinct creation— A play filled with exceptionally rich and hearty portraitures."—*New York Herald-Tribune*.

"Wit, perception and the fine Italian hand of the artist has written this play of tattered nobility and horrible, hypocritical rascals. Epigram plays over it like intellectual lightning— Through it runs the genuine current of human nature."—*The Outlook*.

SOMETHING NEW!

"You folks who go to the theatre only once or twice a week, and therefore have to watch the same old Punch and Judy dolls of modern drama come bobbing up and go flopping down only seventy-five or eighty times a season, do not realize what a play like 'Children of Darkness' means to us old lifers. It is almost like seeing our first play in the theatre. For in 'Children of Darkness,' Edwin Justus Mayer has not only revolutionized the theatre by peopling his play with new characters, so new that you cannot actually foretell what they are going to do next, but he has given them fresh speeches to utter and, what is even more incredible, speeches with a genuine literary quality which will bear inspection on the printed page."—Robert Benchley—*The New Yorker*.

"Edwin Justus Mayer's 'Children of Darkness' is a welcome relief from most of the drip that the stage has been disgorging this season. It has dignity; it has some respect for the beauty of the English language; and it aims at something higher than the level of the box office till— The exhibit as a whole may be recommended to anyone whose ear is tickled by a skillful and fanciful pen."—George Jean Nathan—*Judge*.

" 'Children of Darkness' is exceptional, a distinguished play of thought and feeling, wit and intelligence."—*The Graphic*.

"Even with its tickling caviar flavor, 'Children of Darkness' has enough of the good strong odor of corned beef and cabbage to reach that part of the dear public which forms box office queues. I found it a rare evening of distinguished playwrighting, playacting, and play production."—Fannie Hurst.

"An unusual, brilliant, distinguished piece of work."—Theresa Helburn.

"To be delighted no matter how, is—delightful. To be delighted intellectually and artistically is gorgeous. 'Children of Darkness' is gorgeous."—Rupert Hughes.

" 'Children of Darkness' is a brilliant play."—Roland Young.

"There is a light of hope for the American theatre after all, when Americans can write, act and stage as picturesque and brilliant a comedy as 'Children of Darkness.' "—Robert E. Sherwood.

"I thoroughly enjoyed 'Children of Darkness.' Its writing and characterizations are highly distinguished."—Lawrence Langner.

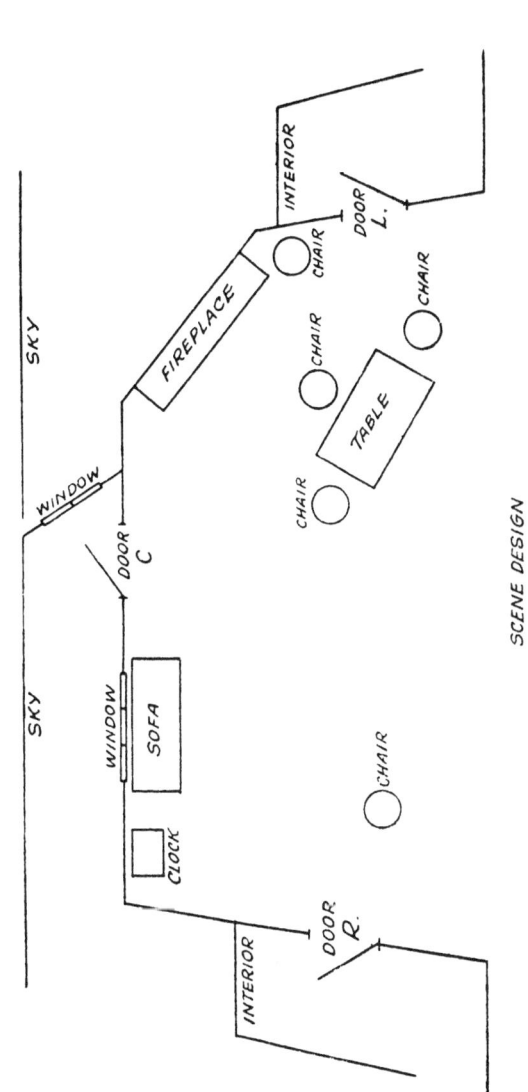

SCENE DESIGN

"CHILDREN OF DARKNESS"

www.ingramcontent.com/pod-product-compliance
Lightning Source LLC
Chambersburg PA
CBHW070635120726
47909CB00004B/1442